Beautiful Stranger

The Ghost of Kate Morgan and the Hotel del Coronado

Beautiful Stranger

The Ghost of Kate Morgan and the Hotel del Coronado

The official account of Kate Morgan's 1892 visit
and why she haunts The Del today

Hotel del Coronado Heritage Department
Coronado, California

First printing October 2002

Printed in the United States of America.

Published by
Hotel del Coronado Heritage Department
1500 Orange Avenue
Coronado, CA 92118
619-435-6611
www.hoteldel.com

Photography provided by Shelley Metcalf

Copies may be ordered from:
Hotel del Coronado Retail Department
1500 Orange Avenue
Coronado, CA 92118
888-236-1357
Or on our Web site: www.hoteldel.com

Other books by the Hotel del Coronado
Hotel del Coronado: An American Treasure With a Storybook Past, 2001

Publisher's Notes

We have made every effort to include only factual and verifiable information in providing as complete an account as possible of Kate Morgan's life and death. If you know of any facts that conflict with the information provided here, or if you can provide additional information, please contact:

Heritage Department
Hotel del Coronado
1500 Orange Avenue
Coronado, CA 92118
619-435-6611
www.hoteldel.com

Special thanks to:
San Diego Historical Society
San Diego Public Library
San Diego State University
Save Our Heritage Organisation

And to all our guests who have shared their "ghost stories" with us.

Contents

Chapter 1

Introduction to the Kate Morgan Story

Kate Morgan as a Guest of the Hotel

Kate Morgan, a pretty woman in her mid-20s, checked into the Hotel del Coronado on Thursday, November 24, 1892, registering under the alias of "Lottie A. Bernard" (from Detroit). Five days later, on November 29, Kate was found dead on a hotel exterior staircase leading to the beach. She had a gunshot wound to her head, which the San Diego County coroner later determined was self-inflicted.

Because the police found nothing to positively identify Kate Morgan as Lottie A. Bernard (aside from her registering under that name), a description of Kate and the circumstances of her death were telegraphed to police agencies around the country. The San Diego police also made a sketch of Kate's face, which was sent to the nation's newspapers. Meanwhile, the local press began to refer to Kate as the "Beautiful Stranger."

Eventually, the San Diego coroner received a letter from an unknown source identifying Lottie A. Bernard as Kate Morgan, originally from Iowa and the wife of Tom Morgan, a gambler. This letter provided the authorities with the name of Kate's grandfather, Joe W. Chandler, who lived in Riverton, Iowa, and it suggested that the police contact him to claim Kate's body.

Once it was revealed that Kate had used an alias, speculation soon followed. Adding fuel to the fire was the fact that Kate had been traveling alone (something women generally did not do in 1892) and had arrived at the Hotel del Coronado without any luggage. It was even speculated that Kate may have been pregnant, unmarried and deserted. Under these circumstances, and with possibly nowhere else to turn (or so the stories went), Kate made the decision to end her life. Although this is a possible scenario, it isn't necessarily an accurate one. In fact, an autopsy was never performed on Kate's body, and to this day, Kate's health at the time of her death is unknown.

The coroner's inquest, which tried to determine the circumstances of Kate's life and her death, was held on November 30, 1892. This was the day after Kate's body was found, and before much was known about her. As a result, the inquest is rather sketchy (especially by today's standards); some of the information in this official report is even in error. Still, witness testimony provided a very vivid account of Kate's behavior during her final days at The Del.

Among other things, the inquest revealed that Kate appeared to have been extremely sickly and despondent. In fact, Kate had told hotel employees that she was suffering from stomach cancer (the newspapers would later use this information to support the pregnancy theory, speculating that stomach cancer and pregnancy could cause similar symptoms). Despite her ill health, however, Kate instructed the hotel staff not to worry about her, and added that her brother, a doctor, would be arriving any day.

In fact, during her stay at The Del, Kate approached the front desk again and again to ask about her brother's impending visit (had he arrived yet, and if not, had he sent word), but hotel staff would later testify that Kate had received no messages or visitors during her stay. (According to family records, Kate didn't even have a brother, but this fact wasn't revealed at any point during the 1892 investigation and really didn't play a part in the story at that time.)

Kate had also told the hotel staff that this same brother had been traveling with her from Los Angeles to San Diego but had to leave the train unexpectedly in the city of Orange. In the process, according to Kate, her brother had inadvertently taken all the baggage claim checks with him, leaving Kate with no way to retrieve her luggage upon reaching San Diego. This, Kate had explained, was why she checked into The Del without any bags. (After her death, the police were never actually able to locate any luggage that could be traced to Kate Morgan.)

Only after the inquest had been completed did a gentleman come forward to corroborate some of Kate's story. As it was later reported by the newspapers, this man, Joseph E. Jones, said he had traveled to San Diego in the same railcar with Kate and her male companion. Jones reported that the couple had had a bitter quarrel, and that the gentleman had gotten off the train in Orange; Kate, meanwhile, continued to San Diego.

Based on the fact that this argument appeared to be more of a lovers' quarrel than a sibling standoff, Jones came to the conclusion that the gentleman with Kate was probably her husband – or, worse yet, her lover. And out of Kate's despair for having been abandoned, she decided to kill herself.

Although Jones' eyewitness account appears to be credible, it does fall apart in a critical way: Jones claims he traveled from Denver with Kate Morgan. The fact is, as far as can be determined, Kate Morgan started her trip to The Del from Los Angeles, where she had been living at the time (although there are about 24 "travel" hours unaccounted for: Kate left Los Angeles on the day before Thanksgiving and didn't arrive at the Hotel del Coronado until Thanksgiving Day. In that a train ride from Los Angeles to San Diego wouldn't have required more than a day's time, where had Kate been all that time?).

Eventually, newspapers revealed more about Kate's true identity (but not before she had been misidentified twice as other missing women). It was ultimately determined that at the time of her death, Kate had been living and working as a domestic at the Los Angeles residence of L.A. Grant, where she had used the name "Katie Logan." While in Los Angeles, Kate had sometimes talked about her husband, Tom, but admitted that he was not in Los Angeles and that she "did not know what had become of him."

According to later newspaper stories, it was reported that Kate had also shared with coworkers her concerns about Tom's gambling, saying that she "was not happy with him." For her part, Kate was described as a model employee, who "bore an excellent reputation. She attended strictly to her duties all the time and was never out at night, and so far as is known, she did not have any men around her the whole time she was here."

In fact, on the day Kate left Los Angeles to travel to The Del, her employer had no idea that she would not be returning. On the contrary, Kate was expected to be back the next day, which would have been Thanksgiving Day, to help with the household's holiday preparations. Perhaps even Kate hadn't realized she'd never return to Los Angeles, because she left behind what seemed to be some of her most important and sentimental personal belongings. From all appearances, it looked as if Kate had intended to return to her life in Los Angeles.

~

Kate Morgan as the Ghost of the Hotel

Kate's worldly possessions weren't the only things she left behind; many people believe that Kate Morgan also left her spirit. The fact is, stories about the ghost of Kate Morgan have circulated since her death.

Though reports of ghostly sightings may have started immediately after Kate's death (ghosts were a big topic of conversation at the turn of the century), it is unlikely that the hotel would have wanted them made public. On the contrary, even as late as the 1960s, The Del was trying to keep a tight lid on any ghostly goings-on. In fact, according to internal correspondence from that time, the hotel was very clear about its desire to keep the ghost story under wraps. Unfortunately, in The Del's absence, others stepped forward to tell their own tales – often with unbelievable results!

Because of the misinformation being circulated, the hotel began to research Kate's life, her death – and her "ghost." Newspapers and the coroner's inquest provided a lot of information about Kate the person (as it was reported in her time); personal interviews with guests and hotel personnel, in turn, provided a lot of information about Kate the ghost (as it is reported in our time).

Today it is believed that the ghost of Kate Morgan haunts the guestroom that Kate occupied in 1892. (The numbering of the rooms in the Victorian Building has changed a few times since the hotel first opened; as a result, the 1892 room that Kate stayed in – Room 302 – is today Room 3327.) Although many ghosts are characterized as scary or even mischievous, Kate's ghost is distinguished by a benign and gloomy sadness.

Guests, housekeepers and other hotel employees (some of whom are unwilling to work in "Kate's Room" by themselves) have reported unusual activity in Room 3327, including flickering lights, a television that turns on and off by itself, breezes coming from nowhere, strange scents and sounds, items moving on their own, doors that randomly open and close, abrupt changes in room temperature, and the sound of unexplained footsteps and voices. Still other guests and employees claim to have seen the ghost of Kate Morgan herself.

Independent paranormal researchers, in turn, have documented supernatural activity using high-tech gadgetry, including infrared cameras, night vision goggles, radiation sensors, toxic-chemical indicators, microwave imaging systems and high-frequency sound detectors. In the process, these investigators have recorded mysterious temperature fluctuations, magnetic fields, electronic emissions and other unexplained phenomena.

But Kate Morgan's ghost is only one part of Kate's story. The story really begins with Kate Morgan herself – and with her mysterious death at The Del in 1892. The next chapter explores Kate's final days.

CHAPTER 2

Kate Morgan's Last Days at The Del:

A Chronology Based on the Coroner's Inquest Testimony

The Coroner's inquest, which was conducted on November 30, 1892 (the day after Kate's body had been discovered), contained a lot of firsthand information. From this, it is possible to piece together a detailed account of Kate's final days.

Unfortunately, in some places, the inquest testimony tends to be incomplete or even in error. Even so, what follows is as accurate a timeline as possible, based upon all the information contained in the original report. The information that follows, however, has been rearranged chronologically and is in narrative form.

A verbatim copy of the inquest – which does not proceed chronologically and is in the form of a trial transcript, witness by witness – is included in Chapter 3.

To help keep the Kate Morgan story straight, a list of all the people involved is included below.

Who's Who

THE DECEASED

~ **Lottie Anderson Bernard:** Alias used by Kate Morgan (although no one at the inquest realized this was an alias until after the interviews had been completed)

WITNESSES

~ **M. Chick:** Owner/Gunsmith/Gun Dealer, Chick's Gun Shop, 1663 Sixth Street, San Diego

~ **David Cone:** Electrician at the Hotel del Coronado; Cone resided at the hotel

~ **T.J. Fisher:** Sold real estate out of an office in the Hotel del Coronado's drugstore; also resided at the hotel

~ **A.S. Gomer:** Clerk, Hotel del Coronado

~ **Frank Heath:** Clerk, Ship Chandlery Store, 624 Fifth Street, San Diego; resided at 1516 Union Street, San Diego

~ **F.W. Koeppen:** Gardener at the Hotel del Coronado; resided in Coronado, possibly at The Del

~ **B.F. Mertzman:** Physician and Surgeon, Fifth Street, San Diego; resided at Twenty-second and E streets, San Diego

~ **H.J. Stetson:** Deputy Coroner, San Diego

~ **W.P. Walters:** Bystander in Chick's Gun Shop

~ **Harry West:** Bellboy at the Hotel del Coronado; resided between Sixteenth and Seventeenth, on I, in San Diego

ADDITIONAL NAMES

~ **Johnson & Company:** Undertakers, 907 Sixth Street, San Diego

- **Mr. Fosdick:** The pharmacist who ran the hotel's drugstore
- **Mr. Green:** Probably a hotel employee (he accompanied T.J. Fisher when Fisher went to look at Kate's body after it had been discovered on an exterior hotel staircase)
- **Mr. Rossier:** Assistant Manager at the Hotel del Coronado

THURSDAY, NOVEMBER 24, 1892

Afternoon: According to the hotel's guest register, this is the day Kate Morgan checked in (although she did not check in under her own name; she used the alias Lottie Bernard). Arriving in the afternoon, Kate did not sign the guest register herself; a hotel clerk signed in for her.

Evening: The clerk (name unknown) who had registered Kate had told another hotel clerk, A.S. Gomer, that a "rather peculiar person" had arrived in the afternoon. Later that evening, the same clerk pointed out Kate to Gomer.

At about this time, Kate began a series of conversations with Harry West, the bellboy who attended her throughout her stay. Kate told West that she was sick with "neuralgia" (a general term used to refer to nerve pain or spasms). Kate also told West that she was expecting her brother to "come down" and join her at the hotel (although, as far as can be determined, Kate had no brother).

FRIDAY, NOVEMBER 25, 1892

Morning: On the morning after she checked in, Kate approached A.S. Gomer about retrieving her baggage, which she said had been left at the train station in San Diego. According to Kate, she and her brother (who she said had been traveling with her) had become separated in Orange, California. Although Kate had continued the trip to San Diego, her brother had not.

Not only was Kate uncertain about where her brother had finally ended up, she was also concerned because he had inadvertently taken her baggage claim checks with him. Kate told Gomer that her brother's name was Dr. Anderson, and that he would be arriving that day (Gomer later testified that Kate had asked him every day thereafter whether or not her brother had arrived).

SATURDAY, NOVEMBER 26, 1892

Time not known and day may be uncertain (T.J. Fisher referred to the day as "about last Saturday"): On the second day of her stay, Kate went into the hotel's drugstore and walked around slowly, appearing to be sick and in pain. Kate asked T.J. Fisher (who ran a real estate office out of the drugstore) if he could give her something for her suffering. Fisher referred her to Mr. Fosdick, the manager of the drugstore; Fosdick suggested Kate see a physician. According to Fisher, Kate told Fosdick not to worry, mentioning that her brother was a physician and that he would be joining her soon. (Interestingly, Fosdick did not testify at Kate's inquest.)

Time uncertain: Later that day, Kate asked bellboy Harry West to go to the hotel drugstore for her, and to bring her back an "empty pint bottle" and a sponge.

SUNDAY, NOVEMBER 27, 1892

According to the inquest transcript, no activity involving Kate Morgan had been reported on this day.

MONDAY, NOVEMBER 28, 1892

Time uncertain: On Monday, Kate sent bellboy Harry West to the bar twice – once for a glass of wine and once for a "whiskey cocktail." West then "fixed" a bath for Kate and brought her a pitcher of ice water. Kate told West that she was going to be in the bath for an hour or two.

About noon: After her bath, Kate rang for West and asked him to dry her hair (apparently this kind of personal service was commonplace at that time). Kate explained that she had inadvertently fallen into the tub and had gotten her head wet. West thought Kate appeared to be "suffering a great deal ... she groaned a great deal, and slept most of the day ... she would sleep a little while, and then wake up, and be groaning ... she looked pale in the face." Kate again mentioned to West that she was expecting her brother to join her.

Sometime between noon and 1 p.m.: West reported to clerk A.S. Gomer that he had just delivered a whiskey to Kate. Gomer, who had already been concerned about Kate's health (he had asked a housekeeper to talk to her about seeking medical care), went up to Kate's room to try to convince her to see a doctor. After Kate refused, Gomer tried to convince Kate to light a fire in the fireplace (Gomer testified that "it was a very gloomy, dreary sort of a day"), but Kate refused that, too.

Kate then explained to Gomer that she already knew what was wrong with her – stomach cancer – and that the doctors had already given up on her, calling her case "hopeless." Kate also told Gomer that her brother, "Doctor Anderson," practiced medicine in Indianapolis and would be joining her soon (Gomer added that he had found Kate's story to be very credible up until this point).

Even so, Gomer was nonetheless concerned about Kate's ability to pay her bill (Kate had been charging all of her hotel expenses to her room account, which she wouldn't be expected to pay until she checked out). As a result, Gomer asked Kate if she was traveling with enough "funds," which he pointed out, would definitely be needed in her present condition. In reply, Kate told Gomer to send a telegram to a G.L. Allen, in Hamburg, Iowa, and that Mr. Allen would provide the funds. (Although funds reached the hotel the day Kate's body was found, it was left to the newspapers to speculate about the identity of G.L. Allen and his connection to Kate.)

Sometime in the afternoon: Later that same day, Kate "rang" for some matches (her call was presumably answered by bellboy Harry West). West offered to go get her a whole box of matches, or even to give Kate the few matches he had in his own pocket. At that point, Kate told West that she just needed to burn some papers in the fireplace.

Afternoon: Kate returned to the hotel's drugstore. T.J. Fisher, the real estate agent, noticed that Kate walked very slowly and appeared to be in great pain. At some point, Kate must have told Fisher that she was planning to travel to San Diego because he said to her, "It seems too bad for you to go over in town and you suffering from neuralgia, in this stormy weather." Kate responded, "I am compelled to go. I forgot my checks [baggage claim checks], and I have got to go over and identify my trunks, personally."

Between 4 and 5 p.m.: That same day, Kate traveled by train from the Hotel del Coronado to downtown San Diego. Her first stop was the Ship Chandlery [Specialty] Store (624 Fifth Street), where she asked the clerk, Frank Heath, if he sold revolver cartridges. Kate appeared to be nervous and excited. Said Heath, "She spoke to me three or four times before I could understand her; she spoke so low." Kate also appeared to be sick – she walked very slowly – and looked "very bad" (although Heath did note that Kate was well dressed). Because Heath's store did not sell revolver cartridges, he directed her to Chick's Gun Shop (although, after Kate left his store, Heath didn't actually see where she went).

About 3 p.m.: Even though Frank Heath had testified that Kate had come into his store between 4 and 5 p.m. (before going on to Chick's Gun Shop at 1663 Sixth Street), M. Chick testified that Kate had come into his store at about 3 p.m. Upon entering the shop, Kate told Chick that she wanted to buy a gun as a Christmas present for a friend. Chick sold her a pistol and some cartridges, and he showed her how to load it. Kate and Chick also discussed how hard it was to use, after which Kate took her packages and left. (At the inquest, however, when pressed to "positively" identify the corpse of Kate as the woman who had come into his store, Heath was unable to do so.)

Also in the gun shop was bystander W.P. Walters. Walters thought Kate appeared to be very odd, walking very slowly. After Kate left, Walters remarked to an unidentified bystander, "That woman, she is going to hurt herself with that pistol." Walters said that the bystander agreed with this assessment.

From the gun shop, Kate walked south on Fifth Street, heading toward Schiller & Murtha's at Fifth Street and D Avenue. According to Walters, this was as far as he could see, although he guessed that Kate might have also stopped at the Combination (probably another retail establishment).

After her purchases were made, Kate returned to the hotel by train.

6:30 p.m.: After dark, bellboy Harry West saw Kate on a second-floor hotel veranda, which overlooked the ocean. This was on the opposite side of the building from Kate's room. According to West, this was the last time he saw Kate.

Between 7 and 8 p.m.: Later that evening, Kate went to clerk A.S. Gomer's office to ask one last time if there had been any letters or telegrams for her. Gomer told Kate there weren't any; this was the last time Gomer saw Kate. In fact, this was the last time anyone who testified at the inquest would see Kate alive.

TUESDAY, NOVEMBER 29, 1892

7:30 a.m.: The following morning, Kate's body was found at the west oceanfront corner of the hotel, on an exterior staircase leading to the beach (this location, however, would be repeatedly misidentified as the "north" corner of the building). Kate was discovered lying on the steps, feet toward the ocean, by David Cone, a hotel electrician, while he was "trimming" the exterior lights. Nearby there was blood on the steps and a "large pistol" to her right. Cone described Kate's clothes as being "all wet, and the body seemed to have been lying there quite awhile, to have been dead quite awhile."

As Cone left the area to report what he had found, he encountered F.W. Koeppen, a hotel gardener. Cone told Koeppen about his discovery, and together they returned to the scene. After looking over the situation, Koeppen went to notify Mr. Rossier, the hotel's assistant manager. Cone, in the meantime, went to the office to inform the chief clerk. Afterward, Cone returned to finish trimming the lights. Koeppen, meanwhile, returned to the scene with Rossier, and the two men covered Kate's body with a canvas. Koeppen remained with Kate until the San Diego coroner removed her body later that morning.

8:30 a.m.: T.J. Fisher, the real estate agent whose office was in the hotel drugstore, also saw Kate's body after her death; Fisher was accompanied to the scene by a Mr. Green, probably another hotel employee. At the inquest, Fisher speculated that no one had heard the gunshot that killed Kate because "at the north, north corner, the surf probably would deaden the noise." (In reality, the location to which Fisher referred was the west oceanfront corner of the building.)

Morning, "as soon as the office opened": Meanwhile, the same day that Kate's body was found, hotel clerk A.S. Gomer received a telegram from a bank in Hamburg, Iowa, extending $25 credit to "Lottie A. Bernard." Gomer sent a reply, informing the bank that Lottie A. Bernard (who would later be identified as Kate Morgan) "had suicided" and that the bank should contact the coroner in San Diego for more information

Morning: Summoned by telegraph sent soon after Kate's body had been discovered, H.J. Stetson, San Diego's deputy coroner, arrived to view the scene, sometime between 9:30 and 10 a.m. Stetson estimated that Kate had been dead for about six or seven hours (this would mean that Kate had killed herself early on November 29, and not late on the November 28). The undertakers came "over [on] the next boat," to take Kate's body back to their San Diego establishment, Johnson & Company (907 Sixth Street).

Afterward, Stetson searched Kate's room, where he found, among other things, a valise (suitcase), night dress, hat, penknife, handkerchiefs, some bottles – one with camphor (this could have been used topically to relieve pain), one with alcohol (Stetson conjectured that this might have been brandy), as well as some quinine pills (these could have been taken to reduce fever) – and a purse containing a small ring, the key to Kate's valise and $16.50, although nothing "that would throw any identity upon where she was from."

In addition, Stetson found some puzzling papers in Kate's room, along with a monogrammed handkerchief. He noted that Kate's bed "had not been touched at night," and added that it looked as if Kate had burned some papers in the fireplace.

WEDNESDAY, NOVEMBER 30, 1892

Time unknown: On November 30, 1892, the coroner's inquest was held.

At some point previous to the inquest, Dr. B.F. Mertzman, a physician and surgeon, had been called to the undertakers, Johnson & Company, to examine Kate's body. Mertzman would later testify that Kate had been killed by a single bullet to her right temple, and that the wound was consistent with the type of gun found by Kate's body.

Chapter 3

The Coroner's Report:

The Official Account of Kate Morgan's Death

Inquisition by Coroner's Jury

~

In the matter of the Inquisition upon the Body of

Lottie Anderson Bernard

a.ka. Kate Morgan

Deceased

November 28, 1892

Date of death

State of California
County of San Diego

To aid in the positive identification of Kate Morgan, the police circulated a sketch of her face.

The inquest into Kate Morgan's death was conducted on Wednesday, November 30, 1892, the day after her body was found. Although the inquest provides detailed information, with careful reading, it is clear that some of the testimony is contradictory, and in some places critical questions were never asked. Because of this, it is easy to see why so much remains uncertain about Kate's life and death.

Note also that according to the coroner's inquest, Kate died on Monday, November 28, 1892. Her death certificate, however, gives Kate's date of death as November 29, 1892. Kate's body was actually found on Tuesday, November 29, but no official time of death was ever established.

In addition, although some witnesses testified that Kate's body was found at the northern corner of the building ("towards Point Loma ... next to the ocean"), this was actually the western oceanfront corner of the building. Directions in Coronado are frequently given in error due to the fact that the beach tends to run east-west – and not north-south as one would expect (the West Coast, overall, does have a north-south orientation). Even today, this is a common mistake due in part to the fact that North Island Naval Air Station is not really north of the village of Coronado, but west of it.

1892 Calendar

November/December

Sun	Mon	Tues	Wed	Thurs	Fri	Sat
Nov 20	21	22	23	24	25	26
27	28	29	30	Dec 1	2	3
4	5	6	7	8	9	10
11	12	13	14	15	16	17

Key Players

~ **The Deceased, Lottie Anderson Bernard:** Alias used by Kate Morgan (although no one at the inquest realized this was an alias until after the interviews had been completed)

~ **W.A. Sloane, Esq.:** Justice of the Peace and Acting Coroner

~ **W.W. Whitson:** Recorder and transcriber of inquest proceedings

JURORS

~ **William Cooper**

~ **L. Dampf**

~ **J.S. Dowd**

~ **Milton Lamb**

~ **Frank Kemmer**

~ **T.J. McCord**

~ **A.T. Randall**

~ **J.M. Spencer**

~ **E.A. Stevens**

WITNESSES

~ **M. Chick:** Owner/Gunsmith/Gun Dealer, Chick's Gun Shop, 1663 Sixth Street, San Diego

~ **David Cone:** Electrician at the Hotel del Coronado; Cone resided at the hotel

~ **T.J. Fisher:** Sold real estate out of an office in the Hotel del Coronado's drugstore; also resided at the hotel

~ **A.S. Gomer:** Clerk, Hotel del Coronado

~ **Frank Heath:** Clerk, Ship Chandlery Store, 624 Fifth Street, San Diego; resided at 1516 Union Street, San Diego

~ **F.W. Koeppen:** Gardener at the Hotel del Coronado; resided in Coronado, possibly at The Del

~ **B.F. Mertzman:** Physician and Surgeon, Fifth Street, San Diego; resided at Twenty-second and E streets, San Diego

~ **H.J. Stetson:** Deputy Coroner, San Diego

- **W.P. Walters:** Bystander in Chick's Gun Shop
- **Harry West:** Bellboy at the Hotel del Coronado; resided between Sixteenth and Seventeenth, on I Street, in San Diego

ADDITIONAL NAMES

- **Johnson & Company:** Undertakers, 907 Sixth Street, San Diego
- **Mr. Fosdick:** The pharmacist who ran the hotel's drugstore
- **Mr. Green:** Probably a hotel employee
- **Mr. Rossier:** Assistant Manager at the Hotel del Coronado

The verbatim transcript below has not been edited.

~

The Inquest Transcript

Inquisition by coroner's jury in the matter of the Inquisition upon the Body of Lottie Anderson Bernard, aka Kate Morgan [Kate's actual identity – as Kate Morgan and not Lottie Anderson Bernard – was not discovered until the inquest testimony had been completed; it is likely that the inquest transcript was not released to the public until Kate's true identity, "aka Kate Morgan," could be determined and inserted here], Deceased, State of California, County of San Diego, November 28, 1892 date of death [on Kate's "Certificate of Death," her death is listed as November 29, 1892]. Over the body of Lottie Anderson Bernard, Deceased, before W.A. Sloane, Esq., Justice of the Peace and Acting Coroner.

The Coroner orders W.W. Whitson to report in short hand and transcribe the testimony and proceedings herein.

San Diego, California, Wednesday, November 30, 1892. The following named gentlemen were called, and sworn to act as jurors in this inquisition, viz: E.A. Stevens, T.J. McCord, Frank Kemmer, William Cooper, A.T. Randall, J.S. Dowd, J.M. Spencer, L. Dampf and Milton Lamb.

~

DAVID CONE is called, and testifies as follows (not being sworn at this time):

By Acting Coroner Sloane: *What is your name?*
Cone: *David Cone.*

Coroner: *Where do you live?*
Cone: *At the Hotel del Coronado, Coronado Beach.*

Coroner: *Were you at the Hotel del Coronado night before last, and yesterday morning?*
Cone: *Yes sir.*

Coroner: *Do you know any of the facts in relation to the finding of the dead body about the hotel?*
Cone: *I believe I was the first one to find it.*

Coroner: *State the facts in reference to the discovery of the body.*
Cone: *Every morning I commence at seven o'clock to trim the electric lights around the hotel. Yesterday morning at half past seven I was trimming the electric light at the north corner of the hotel, and when I came to the pole I was just going to climb the pole, I saw the body lying on the stone steps right close to the pole.* [By "trimming" the lights, Cone was probably just turning them off manually.]

Coroner: *Where abouts? What portion of the hotel was that?*
Cone: *I think it is the north corner, it is the corner of the hotel towards Point Loma* [the corner Cone references is actually the western corner of the building].

By a Juror: *Next to the ocean?*
Cone: *Next to the ocean.*

Coroner: *You say you found a body there?*
Cone: *Yes sir.*

Coroner: *Who was it, do you know?*
Cone: *I have no idea.*

Coroner: *Man or woman?*
Cone: *Woman.*

Coroner: *What was the condition of it?*
Cone: *It was lying on the steps, with its feet towards the ocean, head on the steps, almost on the top step. There was blood on the step. The clothes were all wet, and the body seemed to have been lying there quite awhile, to have been dead quite awhile.*

Coroner: *The person was dead?*
Cone: *Yes sir.*

Coroner: *Did you find any weapons there?*
Cone: *There was a large pistol lying at the right-hand side of the body.*

Coroner: *Did you discover any wounds on the person?*
Cone: *No sir.*

Coroner: *You say there was blood?*
Cone: *Yes sir, on the steps, on the right-hand side.*

Coroner: *Have you seen the remains that are at the undertaking establishment of Johnson & Company in this City, at the present time?*
Cone: *I have, yes sir.*

Coroner: *Was it the same person whose body you found?*
Cone: *It is, to the best of my knowledge.*

Coroner: *You say you do not know who that woman was?*
Cone: *I never saw her until I ---*

Coroner: *Who else was present?*
Cone: *No one else.*

Coroner: *What did you do when you found it?*
Cone: *I started towards the office to report, when I had not gone very far, when I met the gardener* [F.W. Koeppen]. *I showed him the body, and I started off again to the office. I went to the office this time, and informed the chief clerk. Then I went back and trimmed the light at the corner, and went on about my work. That is all I know of it.*

Coroner: *You said you discovered a pistol lying there. Look at that pistol* (showing pistol to witness) *and see if you have ever seen that before.*
Cone: *I believe there was rust there, when I saw that pistol. That is the rust I saw. Yes, that is the pistol.*

Coroner: *Did you examine it, to see whether or not the chambers had been discharged?*
Cone: *No sir. I did not touch it.*

Coroner: *You did not touch it at all?*
Cone: *No sir.*
(At this time, the witness is sworn, he not having been sworn at the beginning of his testimony, by oversight.)

The reporter reads the testimony as hereinbefore set out, to the witness.

Coroner: *That statement is correct – that is your testimony in relation to the matter, under oath, is it?*
Cone: *Yes sir.*

~

F.W. KOEPPEN, sworn, testifies as follows:

By Acting Coroner Sloane: *Where do you reside?*
Koeppen: *Coronado.*

Coroner: *What is your occupation?*
Koeppen: *Gardener.*

Coroner: *Where were you on the morning of the 29th?*
Koeppen: *Well, in making my rounds, going around the hotel, I met this electrician, Cone. He said there was a dead body lying on the steps. Both together we went down and looked at the body. I said I was going to report it to the management. He went around one way, and I went the other. I met Mr. Rossier* [assistant manager], *and I told him, and both him and I went and looked at the body.*

Coroner: *The first time you saw the body, what did you see there?*
Koeppen: *Nothing, only the dead body lying on the steps. I did not take any notice of it until I went to report it to the management.*

Coroner: *Then you went and got the assistant manager, and returned?*
Koeppen: *Yes sir.*

Coroner: *What examination was made at that time?*
Koeppen: *We both looked at the body, and he suggested to cover it up with some cover. I went to the tool house, and took a canvas and covered it up.*

Coroner: *What position was the body lying in?*
Koeppen: *Lying along on the steps in a sitting position, and after being dead dropped over on the stairway, and I noticed the pistol lying on one side, but I never went close, to see whether it was the same pistol or not.*

Coroner: *Did you notice any wounds?*
Koeppen: *I noticed blood, but I did not see any wounds.*

Coroner: *Is that the pistol?*
Koeppen: *Yes, but I could not identify the pistol.*

Coroner: *It looked like that?*
Koeppen: *Yes, some like that, but I did not touch it.*

Coroner: *Who took charge?*
Koeppen: *It was covered up, until the Coroner came and examined it.*

Coroner: *You were in charge of it then, were you?*
Koeppen: *Yes sir, it was never touched until the Coroner came and took it away.*

Coroner: *Do you know who the person was?*
Koeppen: *No sir, I never saw her in life, except to see her dead body – not to my knowledge.*

Coroner: *Have you seen the remains since her death, since she was brought over here?*
Koeppen: *Yes sir.*

Coroner: *Is it the same person?*
Koeppen: *Yes sir.*

Coroner: *The remains that are here, that were shown to you?*
Koeppen: *Yes sir.*

~

FRANK HEATH, sworn, testifies as follows:

By Acting Coroner Sloane: *What is your name?*
Heath: *Frank Heath.*

Coroner: *Where do you live?*
Heath: *At 1516 Union Street.*

Coroner: *In the city of San Diego?*
Heath: *Yes sir.*

Coroner: *What is your business?*
Heath: *Clerk in the Ship Chandlery Store, 624 Fifth Street.*

Coroner: *Have you seen the remains of the person whose body was viewed by the coroner's jury at Johnson's parlors?*
Heath: *Yes sir, I have.*

Coroner: *Did you see that person in her lifetime?*
Heath: *Yes sir.*

Coroner: *When and where?*
Heath: *I saw her day before yesterday.*

Coroner: *Where was she?*
Heath: *Between four and five.*

Coroner: *Where?*
Heath: *In the store where I am employed.*

Coroner: *What transactions did you have with her?*
Heath: *She asked me if I kept revolver cartridges.*

Coroner: *What did you tell her?*
Heath: *I told her we did not, and directed her where she could get them.*

Coroner: *Did she say anything as to what number she wanted?*
Heath: *No sir, she did not.*

Coroner: *Or size?*
Heath: *No sir.*

Coroner: *Did you have any further conversation with her at all?*
Heath: *No sir. She came in and spoke to me three or four times before I could understand her, she spoke so low. She seemed a little nervous.*

Coroner: *You are sure it is this same person, are you?*
Heath: *To the best of my belief it is.*

Coroner: *How do you identify her, from her appearance, or from her etching?* [A police sketch had been made of Kate's face and sent to newspapers and police departments in the hope that someone would come forward to positively identify the body.]
Heath: *From her appearance.*

Coroner: *You do not know who she was?*
Heath: *No sir, I never saw her.*

Coroner: *Do you know where she went, after she left your place?*
Heath: *No sir, I did not notice.*

Coroner: *Did you have any talk with anybody about her, after she went out?*
Heath: *No, I did not.*

Coroner: *No remarks made about her?*
Heath: *No sir.*

Coroner: *You say at the time she spoke to you it occurred to you that she was nervous and excited?*
Heath: *Yes sir, it did.*

Coroner: *What led you to that conclusion? Why did you form such an opinion as that?*
Heath: *Why, the way she walked and looked.*

Coroner: *How did she walk, and how did she look?*
Heath: *She walked very slow, as if she felt sick, and she looked very bad, in her general appearance. She was well dressed.*

Coroner: *You say you directed her to some place where she could get what she wanted?*
Heath: *Yes sir.*

Coroner: *Where did you direct her?*
Heath: *To Mr. Chick.*

Coroner: *You do not know whether she went there or not?*
Heath: *No sir, I do not.*

~

B.F. MERTZMAN, having been first duly sworn to tell the truth, the whole truth and nothing but the truth, testifies as follows:

By Acting Coroner Sloane: *What is your full name?*
Mertzman: *B.F. Mertzman.*

Coroner: *What is your occupation?*
Mertzman: *Physician and surgeon.*

Coroner: *Where do you reside?*
Mertzman: *Twenty-second and E, and my office is on Fifth Street.*

Coroner: *Were you called to view the remains of the lady who was said to have been found dead at the Hotel del Coronado?*
Mertzman: *Yes sir, I was.*

Coroner: *When was that?*
Mertzman: *About half an hour ago.*

Coroner: *Just recently?*
Mertzman: *Yes sir.*

Coroner: *At what place?*
Mertzman: *At the undertaking establishment of Johnson, on Sixth and E streets.*

Coroner: *You made an examination of the remains there?*
Mertzman: *I made an examination of the remains, and found a gun-shot wound in the right temple region, just between the ear and the out edge of the eyebrow, and about half an inch high up above that line drawn here. The ball entered into the brain, and that is the only opening I could find – no exit at all.*

Coroner: *What direction did the shot enter then, into the head?*
Mertzman: *Well, I took a probe, and it entered almost at an angle about of that* [Mertzman probably used his hand to indicate the angle that the bullet entered].

Coroner: *A little forward and a little upward?*
Mertzman: *A little forward and a little upward, yes sir.*

Coroner: *Are you able to judge what occasioned the wound, can you tell that?*
Mertzman: *It was a gun-shot wound.*

Coroner: *Are you able to judge as to the size of the ball?*
Mertzman: *From the looks of it, I should say about .38 or .40.*

Coroner: *You think it was a ball about the size of that* (handing pistol to witness)*?*
Mertzman: *Yes sir, about the size of that.*

Coroner: *Can you state what was the cause of death?*
Mertzman: *Gun-shot wound in the brain.*

Coroner: *That would have caused death?*
Mertzman: *Yes sir – probably internal hemorrhage.*

By a juror: *You never saw her before, until you saw her awhile ago?*
Mertzman: *I had never seen her before.*

By another juror: *That ball passed through the head, or just remained?*
Mertzman: *Just remained. It went in on the right side, that is all I could see.*

~

T.J. FISHER, sworn, testifies as follows:

By Acting Coroner Sloane: *Your name is T.J. Fisher?*
Fisher: *Yes sir.*

Coroner: *What is your occupation, Mr. Fisher?*
Fisher: *Real Estate.*

Coroner: *Where is your place of business, and residence?*
Fisher: *The Coronado Hotel is my residence, and my place of business is in the hotel drug store.*

Coroner: *Do you know any of the circumstances attending the death of the woman?*
Fisher: *I saw the lady first about last Saturday, when she came into the drug store and walked up and down the floor two or three times; she seemed to be suffering. She asked me if I could get her something to relieve her suffering, and I referred her to Mr. Fosdick, the manager of the store, and Mr. Fosdick advised her to see a physician. She said that her brother was a physician, and that she expected him here. That was the last I saw of her until Monday. On Monday afternoon she came in again, and walked up and down the floor, and looked as though she was still suffering. I said, "It seems too bad for you to go over in town and you suffering from neuralgia in this stormy weather." She said, "I am compelled to go. I forgot my checks* [baggage claim checks], *and I have got to go over and identify my trunks, personally." She went out, and that was the last I saw of her until I saw her dead, lying on the steps.*

Coroner: *Do you know her name?*
Fisher: *Yes sir.*

Coroner: *What is it?*
Fisher: *L.A. Bernard.*

Coroner: *Do you know anything of where she was from?*
Fisher: *No sir, she didn't tell me where she was from. I know nothing more about that than what I saw in the newspaper.*

Coroner: *Is she registered at the hotel as a guest there?*
Fisher: *I guess she was, I did not see her name there.*

Coroner: *You know nothing of her antecedents then?*
Fisher: *Not a thing.*

Coroner: *And the next you saw of her was when she was lying on the steps, dead?*
Fisher: *On the steps, dead.*

Coroner: *What time was that?*
Fisher: *I think that was about half past eight o'clock in the morning.*

Coroner: *Monday morning?*
Fisher: *Yes sir.* [Kate's body was actually found on Tuesday morning.]

Coroner: *Who was present at that time?*
Fisher: *Mr. Green, the young man at the hotel went with me.*

Coroner: *Did you observe anything in connection with the body that had not been testified to here?*
Fisher: *Not a thing, sir.*

Coroner: *Do you know of anyone who does know what time the event of her death occurred?*
Fisher: *No, from the information I could get, nobody seems to know.*

Coroner: *Nobody heard the pistol shot?*
Fisher: *No sir.*

Coroner: *It was near the oceanside, the surf would have a tendency to prevent people from hearing?*
Fisher: *Yes sir, it was at the north, north corner* [Kate's body was actually found at the west oceanfront corner of the building], *the surf probably would deaden the noise.*

By a juror: *You say you knew what her name was?*
Fisher: *Yes sir.*

Coroner: *How did you come to know?*
Fisher: *I was told since; I have seen it in the newspaper.*

Coroner: *That is the only way you know?*
Fisher: *Yes sir.*

By another juror: *The only evidence you have of her malady is her statement?*
Fisher: *That is all, yes sir.*

~

HARRY WEST, sworn, testifies as follows:

By Acting Coroner Sloane: *Your name is Harry West?*
West: *Yes sir.*

Coroner: *Where do you live?*
West: *My folks live between Sixteenth and Seventeenth on I, San Diego – 2519.*

Coroner: *Are you in any employ, in town?*
West: *Yes sir.*

Coroner: *Where are you employed?*
West: *I work at the Hotel del Coronado, bellboy.*

Coroner: *Have you seen the remains of the woman whose body is at the undertaking establishment of Johnson & Company?*
West: *Yes sir.*

Coroner: *Did you ever see her before, alive or dead?*
West: *Yes sir, I saw her alive.*

Coroner: *Saw her in her lifetime, when?*
West: *In her room, where she was sick.*

Coroner: *Where did she room?*
West: *She roomed at the hotel.*

Coroner: *When was that, when did you see her?*
West: *I seen her all the time, until I seen her the last time I seen her was half past six in the evening, that was night before last.*

Coroner: *Sunday evening?*
West: *Yes sir* [the "night before last" was actually Monday evening], *I seen her on the veranda* [West would later testify that he had been assisting Kate in her guestroom at 6:30 on Monday evening, but no one asked him to clarify this later testimony].

Coroner: *Which veranda?*
West: *Second floor.*

Coroner: *Where was her room, what part of the hotel?*
West: *North side.* [This is correct; Kate's guestroom faced north or northeast.]

Coroner: *Do you know where she was found dead?*
West: *Yes sir, I know where she was found dead; I didn't see her.*

Coroner: *Was her room* [Kate's guestroom] *anywhere near there* [where Kate's body had been found]*?*
West: *No sir, it was on the opposite side.* [The opposite side from Kate's northeast-facing guestroom would have been southwest, which is about where her body actually was found.]

Coroner: *Do you know her name?*
West: *No sir.*

Coroner: *Do you know anything about her, any circumstances, or the condition of her health?*
West: *No sir, she only told me that she had the neuralgia very bad, she was very sick; she was expecting her brother to come down.*

Coroner: *Do you know how long she has been at the hotel?*
West: *I think she has been there since the 23rd* [Kate Morgan actually checked in on November 24].

Coroner: *That is your information, which you gathered from others, or is that your recollection of it?*
West: *I seen that upon the register.*

Coroner: *What is your recollection in reference to it, have you been in attendance there as bellboy since that time?*
West: *Yes sir, I have been attending her room, ever since she has been there.*

Coroner: *When was she taken sick?*
West: *She was sick the first day she was there, right along.*

Coroner: *So you attended upon her, constantly?*
West: *Yes sir.*

Coroner: *Did you have any conversation with her, in reference to her sickness?*
West: *No sir, just that she had the neuralgia, that is all.*

Coroner: *Did she send for any medicines or anything?*
West: *Not by me. Let's see, today is the 30th. On the 26th she sent me down to the drug store for an empty pint bottle and a sponge, and that is the only thing she sent me for. She sent me to the bar twice.*

Coroner: *What for?*
West: *Liquors. Sent me once for a glass of wine, and once for a whiskey cocktail. That was day before yesterday* [Monday, November 28, 1892].

Coroner: *That was day before yesterday?*
West: *Yes sir. I fixed her a bath in the morning, and I got her a pitcher of ice water, and she told me she was going to stay in an hour and a half or two hours. About 12 o'clock she rang, and I went up there. Her hair was all wet, and she wanted me to rub it, and I did so. She told me she was so weak, she was standing on the side of the tub and fell into the tub, and got her hair wet, and I rubbed it, and got it dry.*

Coroner: *That was half past six, Sunday evening?*
West: *Yes sir.* [The day was actually Monday – the correction to this testimony is included in the next two questions/answers. Although it appears that West was confirming the fact that he had assisted Kate at 6:30 p.m. in her room, West had already testified that at 6:30 p.m., he had seen Kate for the last time on a second-floor balcony.]

A bystander: *Excuse me – I think the young man means Monday evening* [November 28].

Coroner: *When did the shooting occur?*
West: *Tuesday.* [In reality, it was never officially determined whether Kate had killed herself on Tuesday, or the day before.]

Coroner: *Then that would be Monday evening* [that West last saw Kate]*?*
West: *Yes sir.*

Coroner: *What was her appearance and conduct, did she appear to be suffering from pain?*
West: *Yes sir, she appeared to be suffering a great deal. She groaned a great deal, and slept most of the day. She would sleep a little while, and then wake up, and be groaning. She looked pale in the face.*

Coroner: *She said she expected her brother, did she say where from?*
West: *No sir – she told me where from, but I do not remember the place.*

Coroner: *Do you remember the state?*
West: *No sir.*

By a juror: *What time was it when she sent you for that liquor?*
West: *For the liquor?*

Coroner: *Yes.*
West: *That was day before yesterday* [Monday, November 28, 1892]*, in the morning, about 12 o'clock, somewhere just about 12 o'clock.*

Coroner: *Did you take the money for it?*
West: *No sir, I did not – charged it to the room.*

~

A.S. GOMER, sworn, testifies as follows:

By Acting Coroner Sloane: *What is your name?*
Gomer: *A.S. Gomer.*

Coroner: *What is your occupation?*
Gomer: *I am engaged in the Hotel del Coronado, in the capacity of clerk.*

Coroner: *You are engaged there, and have been for several days past, have you?*
Gomer: *Yes sir, I have been there for six or seven weeks.*

Coroner: *Have you seen the remains that are at the undertaking parlor?*
Gomer: *Yes sir.*

Coroner: *Did you identify them?*
Gomer: *As the person, yes sir, who was stopping there.*

Coroner: *And what is the name?*
Gomer: *Well, the only means, of course, that I have of knowing her name, is the manner in which she was registered.*

Coroner: *What name did she go by?*
Gomer: *Mrs. Lottie A. Bernard, Detroit.*

Coroner: *That is the way she registered, is it?*
Gomer: *She did not register herself. I was not in the office at the time of her arrival, but the young man there registered for her, at her request. That is the name she gave him.*

Coroner: *Is he present?*
Gomer: *No, he is not here.*

Coroner: *You learned that from him subsequently?*
Gomer: *Yes.*

Coroner: *What do you know of her condition and circumstances, during her stay at the hotel?*
Gomer: *Well, all I know is that the young man spoke to me of her arrival, when I came to the office that evening. Said there was rather a peculiar person came in this afternoon, and I asked him to point her out to me, and along between seven and eight o'clock she came along, and he pointed her out, and there was nothing said until the next morning, she came to me, asking my advice as to how she could get her baggage, which she claimed had been checked to San Diego, and the checks* [baggage claim checks] *she said her brother had kept with him, and her brother had been called away from Orange, either to Los Angeles, or Frisco, she in fact did not know where.*

Coroner: *From Orange?*
Gomer: *Yes sir.*

Coroner: *Did she speak of having come here to this place from Orange?*
Gomer: *That is the way her story begun, Orange, she said Orange; her brother was obliged to leave her, to remain there, or go to Frisco, she didn't know which, and that she came on alone from Orange, and that her brother would be along that afternoon. This was the day after her arrival* [the day after Kate's arrival would have been November 25], *and every day she inquired if her brother had arrived. She claimed that her brother was Doctor Anderson, and that the initials were M.C., I'm not sure about that.*

Coroner: *Did she state anything as to where he was, or as to where he had gone?*
Gomer: *She didn't seem to know where he was.*

Coroner: *What do you know of her circumstances financially, whether she was under financial embarrassment?*
Gomer: *After the boy* [bellboy Harry West] *came to the office Monday, and asked for whiskey, I thought it necessary for someone to see her. The housekeeper had been trying to induce her to call the house physician – rather, I insisted that the housekeeper should persuade her to call the house physician, and see just what her condition was, and the housekeeper was unsuccessful; she kept telling the housekeeper that she knew what her trouble was, and that her brother was a physician, and that it was not necessary to call a physician, but after this boy, who has just testified* [bellboy Harry West], *came to the office, and asked for whiskey, and said the lady had fell in the bathtub and wet her hair, I went up to her room myself, and suggested first, that we call the house physician. She was in the bed then, covered up, and she was totally opposed to calling the physician. It was a very gloomy, dreary sort of day, and she was on the east side of the house* [northeast would be more accurate] *without any fire, and I suggested that she have a fire, and be made comfortable. She said no, she was very comfortable, as good as she could expect. She further told me that the doctors had given her up, that she had cancer of the stomach, and that her case was hopeless, but she told us in such an off-hand way that it did not appear suspicious to me, and I endeavored to find out something about her identity. On the table in her room were some letters. I could not find out the contents of them without picking them up, and of course that was out of order. The only thing I saw on the table were some envelopes, addressed to herself, and finally, after I found she was so much opposed to having the physician, I just put the question to her, if she had got her baggage over, and then I asked her if she was supplied with funds; that in her condition she must necessarily need some funds, and she said yes.*
Then I said to her, "Wouldn't it be a good plan to telephone your brother?" She said, "I do not know where to find my brother, I do not know whether he is at Los Angeles, or at Orange, or at Frisco." Then I said, "Is there no one else you could telegraph to for funds," and she suggested the name of G.L. Allen, Hamburg, Iowa, and at her suggestion I wrote a telegram and sent it to Hamburg, and left her then, in the room, that was about

one o'clock, or half past twelve, possibly on Monday [November 28]. *And then the last time I saw her after that, the next time, and last, was that evening about somewhere between seven and eight o'clock, she called at the office ---*

Coroner: *Now what day was this?*
Gomer: *This was on Monday, she called at the office and inquired if there were any letters or telegrams for her. I said, "No, nothing," and went about doing something and that was the last I saw of her until yesterday morning* [November 29], *this man came to me and reported that there was a corpse out on the ocean side of the house, and I immediately went out there, and of course discovered that it was this woman.*

Coroner: *You say you noticed letters addressed to her, on her table?*
Gomer: *Just letters, envelopes, two or three possibly.*

Coroner: *Did you notice the address?*
Gomer: *This same address.*

Coroner: *Lottie A. ---*
Gomer: *Bernard, Detroit.*

Coroner: *Has there been any reply, subsequently, to the telegram?* [This was the telegram sent by the hotel to G.L. Allen in Hamburg, Iowa, at Kate's direction, requesting "funds" to pay for her stay.]

Gomer: *Yes, yesterday morning, as soon as the office opened, a telegram came from Hamburg, Iowa, signed by some bank, but I neglected to bring that telegram with me, and forget the name of the bank – saying that they would honor her draft for $25, show this to the bank. Then I immediately telegraphed to this same party that this person had suicided on the hotel grounds.*

Coroner: *Have you received any reply to that?*
Gomer: *No, and advised them, at the suggestion of one of your assistants here, to telegraph the coroner. We have received no reply. It seems that some time Monday afternoon – in relation to the papers, the memorandum – she rang her bell, and the bell was answered by the boy* [presumably bellboy Harry West], *she asked for a box of matches, but he said if she only wanted a few, he had a few in his pocket. She made the remark that she wished to burn some papers, so that may account for the disappearance of anything of the kind.*

By a juror: *Was there a fireplace in the room?*
Gomer: *Yes sir.*

Coroner: *All those envelopes were postmarked Hamburg, were they?*
Gomer: *No, I saw nothing on her table. She received no mail while she was there. The envelopes I saw were evidently written by herself, and addressed to herself, Mrs. Lottie A. Bernard, without any street address, Detroit – for I was trying if possible to find out who she was.*

Coroner: *You said she said her brother's name was Anderson?*
Gomer: *Yes, Doctor Anderson, and she told me in that conversation that he was a practicing physician in Indianapolis.*

Coroner: *You know nothing of the immediate circumstances of her death?*
Gomer: *Nothing at all, except going there and seeing the body, and returning to the office.*

Coroner: *The house physician there, did he view the body at all?*
Gomer: *The house physician that day was off hunting.*

Coroner: *Are you able to judge in any way as to how long she had been dead at the time she was found?*
Gomer: *Well, no.*

Coroner: *How soon was it before the Coroner reached there, what time of day did he get there?*
Gomer: *I think it was between seven and half past seven that it was reported to me, and I think it was along about half past nine, possibly ten o'clock when the body was removed. I am not sure as to the exact time.*

~

M. CHICK, sworn, testifies as follows:

By Acting Coroner Sloane: *What is your name?*
Chick: *M. Chick.*

Coroner: *Where do you live, Mr. Chick?*
Chick: *At 1663 Sixth Street.*

Coroner: *What is your business?*
Chick: *Gunsmith, gun dealer.*

Coroner: *Have you seen the remains of the woman whose body is at the undertaking parlors of Johnson & Co.?*
Chick: *I have.*

Coroner: *Did you ever see her before?*
Chick: *I think I have.*

Coroner: *If so, under what circumstances, and where?*
Chick: *Well, it is a woman dressed a great deal like the one that came into my store about three o'clock Monday afternoon* [Frank Heath, the clerk in the Ship Chandlery Store, had already testified that Kate had been in his shop on Monday between 4 and 5 p.m. before going to Chick's Gun Shop, but this discrepancy in testimony was never addressed]*, and wanted to look at some pistols; said she wanted to get one, to make a Christmas present to a friend of hers. I showed her the pistols, and she selected one and bought it.*

Coroner: *What kind of a pistol was it?*
Chick: *It was a .44 American bulldog.*

Coroner: *Examine that pistol, will you Mr. Chick?*
Chick: *It was one just like that.*

Coroner: *You would not be able to identify it positively?*
Chick: *No.*

Coroner: *Did you sell her any cartridges?*
Chick: *I sold her two bits' worth of cartridges.*

Coroner: *Did you have any other conversation with her?*
Chick: *None, whatever.*

Coroner: *Was there anything in her appearance that attracted your attention particularly, or in her manner?*
Chick: *Not at all.*

Coroner: *That is all the conversation you had with her upon it?*
Chick: *Yes sir.*

By a juror: *Did you load the pistol for her?*
Chick: *No sir, she asked me how to load it, how it was loaded. I turned the cover back and showed her. I put it in a box for her, she wrapped it up and took it away.*

Coroner: *You, I understand, identified her positively?*
Chick: *No sir, not positively; it looks a great deal like the woman, and like the clothes she wore, but I would not swear it was the same woman.*

~

W.P. WALTERS, sworn, testifies as follows:

By Acting Coroner Sloane: *You have seen the remains of this woman?*
Walters: *Yes sir.*

Coroner: *At the undertaking parlors – have you ever seen her before in her lifetime?*
Walters: *I could not tell, I did not see her face. She walked right past me, within a foot, and very slowly, and was dressed in black, and I noticed particularly that she had on what appeared to me to be a sealskin coat or sack, and rather long.*

Coroner: *Well, you speak of some woman who passed you?*
Walters: *Yes sir, who passed.*

Coroner: *At what time?*
Walters: *On Monday afternoon somewhere along three or four o'clock, I did not know what time it was.*

Coroner: *Where was that?*
Walters: *At Chick's Gun Shop.*

Coroner: *What did she do, in that connection?*
Walters: *She walked right straight past, she came right direct in the door, and walked straight to the showcase, until she came where the pistols were and then she asked for a pistol. Mr. Chick showed her one, she said she did not want a very high-priced one, and she bought the pistol. She asked for some cartridges – that is, the woman who came in there – and then she asked Chick to show her how to load it. He opened the thing, shoved it in, and took it out again. Then she took hold of the pistol, and pulled it, and says, "Isn't this hard to pull?" He said "no," and he took hold of it and pulled "click," "click," "click." She took hold of it again and pulled, and it clicked, and then she asked to have it put in a box, and wrapped up.*

Coroner: *Did you notice anything peculiar about her manner?*
Walters: *Why yes, she came in just as slow, and walked out straight, slow, again, and I remarked I think, that woman – she is going to hurt herself with that pistol. I spoke to the man who was sitting there, and he thought the same thing.*

Coroner: *Do you know where she went from there?*
Walters: *She went south on Fifth Street, and I stepped to the door, and asked a gentleman who was standing at the door where she went and he said she had went into the Combination* [probably another retail establishment], *he thought. I stopped there a few seconds, and then I saw her go straight diagonally across to Schiller and Murtha's* ["dry goods" store at 600-612 Fifth Street], *and that is the last I seen.*

Coroner: *Does the dress this woman wore correspond to that on the person of the deceased?*
Walters: *The clothes I looked at there, yes sir.*

Coroner: *How were the remains dressed?*
Walters: *They had a black dress, and a sealskin sacque* [short jacket] *or coat, or what appeared to me to be a sealskin, I do not know whether it was, and black, and rather long, longer than they usually wear them now.*

Coroner: *That is all you know in relation to the matter?*
Walters: *That is all I know. I did not speak to the lady, she went past me so I did not see her face.*

~

H.J. STETSON, sworn, testifies as follows:

By Acting Coroner Sloane: *You are Deputy Coroner, Mr. Stetson?*
Stetson: *Yes sir.*

Coroner: *Did you receive word yesterday morning that there was a dead person at the Hotel del Coronado, who needed the attention of the coroner?*
Stetson: *I received word to come to Coronado, from the Coronado Hotel. I found the body there.*

Coroner: *What did you do in response to the message?*
Stetson: *I went over and found the body covered, found the lady lying there covered with a tarpaulin. The undertakers came over the next boat, and she was placed in the receiving box and brought to this City, and taken to Johnson's & Company's.*

Coroner: *Did you form any judgment as to how long she might have been dead?*
Stetson: *She laid as though she might have been dead at least six hours – six or seven.* [A.S. Gomer had already testified that the coroner had Kate's body removed sometime between 9:30 and 10 a.m. on the 29th, presumably after at least a cursory examination on his part (lasting a half-hour or so). If Kate had been dead for six or seven hours at that point, as Stetson testifies here, it means Kate had probably killed herself between 2 and 3 a.m. on November 29, 1892 (the date given on Kate's death certificate) and not late on the night of November 28, 1892 (the date stipulated in the inquest).]

Coroner: *She was stiff and cold?*
Stetson: *Yes sir.*

Coroner: *You found the pistol there in the vicinity?*
Stetson: *Yes sir, that pistol was lying on the next step, the stone steps that go down to the surf, and her hand rested on the lower edge of one, and it had fallen out on to the edge of the next one below, and there was blood around and underneath it.*

Coroner: *You superintended the removal of the remains to the undertaking establishment?*
Stetson: *Yes sir.*

Coroner: *And they have been there ever since?*
Stetson: *Yes sir.*

Coroner: *Did you make any examination of the effects in her room?*
Stetson: *Yes sir, I found the things that are right there. I found that valise, and on the table I found this envelope she had addressed.*

Coroner: *Just read it.*
Stetson: *Denman Thompson, the Old Homestead. And "Frank" is written here four times, and "Lottie Anderson Bernard," and "Mrs. Lottie Bernard," "Lottie Anderson Bernard, Detroit," and then on this paper I found "I merely heard of that man, I do not know him." Here is an invitation – here is an invitation to the Hotel del Coronado, signed by Louise Leslie Carter and Lillian Russell.*

Coroner: *What is the name on the handkerchief?*
Stetson: *Little, I think it is, I cannot quite make it out, but the last name is Anderson. She had a purse on her person, that contained $16.50, and there was a little ring in the purse, a plain ring, and the key to her valise.* (Produces ring and purse.)

Coroner: *Nothing else?*
Stetson: *Nothing else, just some ---*

Coroner: *That is the purse, is it?*
Stetson: *Yes sir; that is the purse.*

Coroner: *What other contents were there?*
Stetson: *Just some handkerchiefs.*

Coroner: *Nothing that would throw any identity upon where she was from?*
Stetson: *Not a thing. In the grate in the room it looked as though quite a package of papers had been burned, it was all in ashes, you might say. Whether she had made them for a fire or what they might have been you could not tell, but they had all been burned.*

Coroner: *Any night clothes?*
Stetson: *Just one night dress was hanging in the closet. The bed had not been touched at night. It was all made up; the hat lay on the mantel, a bottle, and penknife. Yes, there was considerable medicine in there, a bottle of camphor and a bottle of alcohol.*

Coroner: *This large bottle here?*
Stetson: *That is brandy, I think, or alcohol, and some quinine pills. Then there is a little piece of paper. I found a piece of paper that had been wrapped around a bottle of some kind. It says if it does not relieve you, you better send for the doctor. It was just signed "Druggist." It did not say where it was from.*

Coroner: *Did you receive information from the Clerk in the hotel, or someone else?*
Stetson: *Yes, I received word – I received a telegram in the morning to come over to Coronado immediately.*

Coroner: *I mean with reference to parties to whom you were to telegraph in reference to her case?*
Stetson: *Yes, Mr. ---*

Coroner: *What was the name, do you remember?*
Stetson: *The gentleman who just left the stand here* [A.S. Gomer], *the clerk there. He telegraphed to I think it was Iowa, to that bank, and to these people to whom she had been writing, I do not know the name, he did the telegraphing. I asked him at the same time to just include for them to telegraph to the coroner, and he said he would, but there has been no reply come.*

Coroner: *You have heard nothing whatever?*
Stetson: *Not a thing, no sir.*

Coroner: *No trace of her friends?*
Stetson: *No sir.*

By a juror: *Have you been to the baggage office, to find out whether she had any there or not?*
Stetson: *No, I have not been to the baggage, but she had no checks or anything put away, to know.*

Coroner [or possibly a juror]: *She said her brother had the checks, but you do not know anything about whether she had baggage?*
Stetson: *No sir, I do not know anything about it, I have not been.*

Coroner: *Have you made any inquiry at all about it to any of the baggage men?*
Mr. Marks [he is not identified]: *No.*

Coroner: *I believe, gentlemen, we have got all the testimony we can get. Unless there is some further inquiry you can suggest, I will submit the case to you. You can take the case and prepare your verdict. Here is a blank. You can fill it out in accordance with the facts.*

The jury, after deliberation, return the verdict which is on file in this matter.

[In script]: I hereby identify that the foregoing transcript contains a full, true and correct settlement of the proceedings had and testimony given in the within mentioned inquisition, and that the said transcript was mislaid while in my possession which is the reason for its not having been heretofore filed. W.W. Whitson

~

Text taken from:
San Diego Historical Society
Research Archives
Coroner's Inquest (RT.69), F59-2.

Chapter 4

The Life and Death of the "Beautiful Stranger":

Annotated Excerpts from the *San Diego Union*'s 1892 Articles

The details surrounding Kate Morgan's mysterious life and death were widely reported in newspapers throughout San Diego, Los Angeles, San Francisco and the rest of the country. These stories held the public's interest for quite a while: Kate's body was found on November 29, newspaper articles started appearing the next day, and coverage continued at least until December 14, two days after Kate Morgan was laid to rest.

Newspaper interest was understandable: Not only had a beautiful, young woman taken her own life at a fashionable resort, she also left behind a series of tantalizing questions: Who was the "Beautiful Stranger"? Where had she come from? And why had she killed herself?

In subsequent days and weeks, details about Kate's short life began to be revealed. Although it is almost impossible to verify these facts today (and Kate left no direct descendants), the news stories do provide a great deal of information about what was reported on Kate's life and her death at that time. It should be noted, however, that newspaper articles did not begin appearing until the inquest had already been concluded. As a result, quite a bit of the information in the newspaper stories does not appear in the inquest, and some of the information is contradictory.

Understandably, the *San Diego Union* (the city's major daily newspaper at the time) published the most articles, but even those are significantly outnumbered by the combined number of articles from other California sources, including two additional San Diego newspapers (the *Daily Bee* and the weekly *Seaport News*), as well as major Los Angeles and San Francisco dailies.

Starting with the *San Diego Union*, however, this is how Kate's story unfolded.

~

SAN DIEGO UNION
Wednesday, November 30, 1892

By Her Own Hand: A Young Woman, Suffering from Incurable Disease, Suicides. She Wanders Out Into the Storm to Die – Desperate Act of a Guest of Hotel del Coronado – A Revolver the Chosen Weapon.

According to this article, Kate – described as "attractive, prepossessing and highly-educated" – was dressed in black with a lace shawl on her head when she was sighted on one of the hotel's oceanside verandas between 9 and 10 on the night of November 28. The article goes on to say that Kate wasn't seen again until 8:20 the following morning, when her body was discovered by the hotel's electrician. By that time, "lashed by the tempest that is sweeping over the whole coast," Kate was "soaking wet, stiff and cold," the storm's heavy rain having "washed away all stains of blood."

Kate was further described as "reserved and ladylike," with "fine clothing," who had checked in on Thanksgiving, carrying no baggage except a small handbag. According to the article, Kate had kept to her room most of the time, but was frequently attended by a housekeeper (however, the housekeeper did not testify at the inquest). According to the housekeeper, Kate had mentioned that she was 24 years old and suffering from cancer of the stomach as well as heart disease.

It was also reported that the housekeeper tried to dissuade Kate from taking a bath on Monday, November 28, "saying it would weaken her" but Kate hadn't been deterred. About an hour later, Kate summoned the bellboy (Harry West, who did testify at the inquest) and asked him to dry her hair. Apparently, the fact that Kate's hair was "drenched to the roots" was so "unusual" in 1892 (when washing one's hair was far from a daily occurrence) that the newspaper termed the dousing an attempt on Kate's part "to commit suicide ... by means of drowning in her bath." By this point, Kate was also being described as "nervous and unstrung." The newspaper article referenced both Kate's physical suffering and her loneliness – "it was understood that she was expecting a brother to arrive at the hotel." When Kate's brother hadn't arrived by Monday, it was speculated that Kate burned her letters and papers and then "went out in the heart of the storm, within fifteen feet of the ocean's edge, and took her life."

Supposedly, Kate left behind "over $20" in her purse as well as an offer of credit from Mr. Allen of Hamburg, Iowa, in the amount of $50 (by the next day, however, the amount of credit extended by Mr. Allen was correctly reported as $25). The newspaper took this as proof that Kate "seemed in no stress for money." Telegrams concerning Kate's death were sent to Mr. Allen and to any potential Bernard relatives in Detroit (which is the city Kate gave as her permanent residence).

~

SAN DIEGO UNION
Thursday, December 1, 1892

Still in Doubt: Identity of the Coronado Suicide as Yet Not Learned. A Possible Clue Contained in a Telegram to Coroner Stetson – Mysterious Disappearance of Her Brother – Various Theories Afloat.

Significant details were included in this day's news that had not been included in the inquest, especially pertaining to Kate's November 28 trip from the Hotel del Coronado into San Diego to purchase a gun. Apparently, Kate left the hotel "shortly after noon Monday," and, traveling by streetcar, asked the conductor for the name of a hardware store. By this time Kate was so weak, she had to be lifted onto the streetcar by the conductor. Kate was given the name "Todd & Hawley [Hardware]," but never actually went there. Then, after purchasing a gun at Chick's Gun Shop, Kate "immediately returned to Coronado, taking the return car with the same conductor."

At 6:30 p.m. on Monday, November 28, Kate checked with the hotel once again to see if "letters or telegrams had come for her or if her brother had come." It was also reported that the handkerchiefs found after Kate's death were embroidered with "Lottie Anderson" and were "of the finest linen."

The article went on to say, "Various theories are entertained by those who have been examining into this most mysterious case. The allusion to her brother by Mrs. Bernard, as she termed herself, and her apparent anxiety to receive advices from him, have led some to believe that there is more in the case than at first sight appears. Is it not possible, nay, probable, that the person to whom she referred as brother entertained a closer relation to this unfortunate woman? they ask." The article argued that a brother would have gotten in touch with the authorities right away, especially since "the news of her suicide was flashed all over the country ... and must have met his eye." The newspaper then posed the question, "Why, then, did he not telegraph at once?"

The article continued, "It is a suspicious circumstance that nothing has been heard from this man. If he had been her lover and had wanted to rid himself of her, he could scarcely have concealed himself more effectually than he has done." This part of the article concluded, "More light will doubtless be cast upon this matter."

~

SAN DIEGO UNION
Thursday, December 1, 1892
A Probable Theory: What a San Diego Physician Thinks of the Suicide.

Kate's death continued to be speculated about in an accompanying article. "For every fact brought out in the investigation of the suicide of the pretty and mysterious stranger at Hotel del Coronado tending to show that the act was done in despondency over sickness, there are dozens of circumstances pointing strongly to the theory that she was betrayed, ruined and deserted, and committed the act soon after the truth dawned upon her."

To help shed light on the mystery, the *San Diego Union* interviewed "a prominent physician, who yesterday [November 30, 1892] examined the body."

"'The girl was about 24 or 25 years old,'" said the doctor. 'Her face bears no trace of intense suffering, and her frame is not wasted, as would be the case if she had been so far gone with cancer as to be pronounced hopeless. But, it is nonsense to say she had cancer of the stomach. Why? Because cancer rarely develops under the age of 40, and I never heard of a case under 35.'"

The doctor's report continued, "'Now look – the first symptoms of pregnancy in certain temperaments and those of cancer of the stomach are almost identical. There is the same great pain in the stomach with sourness and occasional vomiting. The complexion becomes sallow, exactly alike in these cases. I cannot say that the girl was enceinte [a French word meaning pregnant] but the indications I think, point more to that and to an attempt on her part to produce a miscarriage than to long-standing disease. The sallowness of her complexion could very naturally have been made by the strong medicine necessary to effect miscarriage. Again, the dark rings under her eyes, spoken of by the Coronado pharmacist, could have been produced by violent medicine and consequent pain.'"

The unnamed doctor concluded his speculation, "'The indications are that she has already borne a child, and was enceinte when she died, but this cannot be definitely proven without a post-mortem examination. In my opinion she shot herself in desperation over some love affair, as the cases of suicide of females of her age from ill-health are very rare.'"

The doctor also referenced a three-hour horseback ride that Kate was reported to have taken a couple of days after her arrival. "She was noticed by Charles Stevens of the Star Stables, driving a fractious horse, that threatened to run away with her. He proffered his assistance, which she accepted, and he drove with her for several hours. She stopped at Marston's (a department store) and bought a pair of gloves. Throughout the ride, Mr. Stevens says, she was pleasant and companionable, if not actually in high spirits. She certainly did not appear to be in pain, either bodily or mental." The article noted that the gloves purchased at Marston's were not found with Kate's belongings after her death.

In addition, it was reported that Kate had visited the Hotel Brewster in San Diego before checking into The Del on Thanksgiving Day. Apparently, Kate asked about the arrival of her relatives, "Mr. and Mrs. Anderson." Kate was informed that a Mr. and Mrs. Anderson had not yet checked into the Hotel Brewster.

The article concluded, "A deep mystery at present hangs over every act of her mournful tragedy."

~

SAN DIEGO UNION
Friday, December 2, 1892
The Beautiful Stranger: Love Troubles Doubtless Killed Her, But Who Was She? Mystery Deep as Ever Regarding Her Identity – She Quarreled with Her Companion – Her Story Contradictory, But Partially True.

By day three, the *San Diego Union* was reporting more speculation about Kate, her life and her death. "Facts are slowly coming to light to prove the theory that a love-trouble was the cause of the dramatic suicide of Mrs. Lottie Anderson Barnard [the newspaper misspelled Bernard], the beautiful and mysterious stranger who came on Thanksgiving day to Hotel del Coronado. The question of her identity is still unsolved."

Important details were added at this point in Kate's story. Apparently, a bellboy reported that Hotel Del guest Joseph E. Jones of Boston had traveled by train from Denver in the same railcar in which Kate had ridden (although it's unclear which bellboy related this story).

"Mr. Jones said that he had not mentioned the fact, as he was averse to being called to testify before the coroner's jury. He stated that the young woman was accompanied by a well-dressed gentleman. He did not particularly notice the couple until after reaching the coast, when they attracted his attention, and that of others in the car, by high words and bitter quarreling. This they continued at intervals for some time. The quarrel ended with her asking her companion to forgive her, which she repeated several times, but he was obdurate and angry, and at length left the train. Mr. Jones saw no more of her, and thought no more of the matter until he saw her at Hotel del Coronado a day or so afterward. He said he immediately recognized her, and was sure she was the same person."

This article continued to explore the "mysterious" circumstances of Kate's death. "Many persons, noting her familiarity with Los Angeles hotels, and the fact that she was without baggage or funds, believe that she was a Californian, and that the trip to San Diego was a mere escapade." Kate spoke "very familiarly of Los Angeles hotels ... she said her father and mother lived at Detroit, and that the man, G.L. Allen, who was telegraphed to for funds, was in charge of her finances."

The article continued, "The stories told by the lady as to her identity, her companion who left her at Orange, and her baggage are found to be full of contradictions. She gave the bellboy a dollar for a trifling service, and he remonstrated, saying he 'didn't like to take so much from a sick lady.' The boy said she replied, 'Take it; I've got plenty of money.' Yet she had barely $20 in her purse. Altogether her story was inconsistent, contradictory and mysterious."

"It is worthy to remark that G.L. Allen of Hamburg, Iowa, who wired her $25 the same day he received her telegram, has not answered the telegram from Hotel del Coronado announcing her suicide, though three days have elapsed. From this fact the authorities are inclined to believe that he is more than financially interested in the dead girl – in other words, that possibly he had sent her away."

"On the other hand, Mr. Jones' testimony regarding her quarrel on the train strengthens the theory that her companion was her lover instead of her brother, and that he deserted her at Orange. [Mr. Jones never formally "testified" about what he witnessed en route to Coronado; this was reported by the newspaper as hearsay according to a hotel bellboy.] She gave his name as Dr. W.C. or M.C. Anderson, Minneapolis, but no such name is in the directory."

But, still, the "Beautiful Stranger" remained unidentified: "No inquiries have come from any other source, though the facts of the suicide are known all over the United States. In the meantime she lies on a slab in the undertaking rooms, beautiful even in death, the only undoubted fact in all the mystery being that she took her life with her own hand."

~

SAN DIEGO UNION
Saturday, December 3, 1892
A Possible Clue: A Telegram from Detroit Relative to the Coronado Suicide.

Here the newspaper reported a new clue: a telegram had been received by the San Diego chief of police from a Miss May Wyllie in Detroit that read as follows: "Telegraph full description lady's body found on beach. Had short hair, black corset, large-black hat, gold buckle?" Deputy Coroner Stetson pointed out that this description didn't exactly match the description of the corpse, but this one telegram had been the only incoming communication regarding Kate's death. Meanwhile, San Diego police had telegraphed the Farmers' and Merchants' Bank in Hamburg, Iowa, to see if someone there could identify the Mr. G.L. Allen who had wired $25 to Kate.

Following up on Kate's claim that her trunks had been left in San Diego, the police found three trunks at the D Street depot that had come from Omaha, via Denver, but these could not be opened "until proper authorization from the division baggage agent."

~

SAN DIEGO UNION
Sunday, December 4, 1892
Identified: Mrs. Lottie A. Bernard was Lizzie Wyllie of Detroit. In the City of Her Home She was a Book-Bindery Girl. Leaving There Five Weeks Ago in Company with a Married Man. He Who Caused Her to Err was John Longfield, and He was Probably Her Deserter at Orange.

Here, Kate is misidentified as Miss Lizzie Wyllie of Detroit, Michigan. Lizzie's mother, Mrs. Elizabeth Wyllie – with the help of some relatives living in San Diego – confirmed that the dead woman was, indeed, her daughter. As a caveat, however, Lizzie's mother added that the family's San Diego relatives hadn't actually seen Lizzie since she was a little girl, so other relatives from Pasadena were going to travel to San Diego to make the ultimate identification and to "take care of her remains."

According to the article, Lizzie, along with her sister May, had worked at a bookbindery, where Lizzie had become "too intimate with John Longfield," a married man. Ultimately, Lizzie, May and Longfield were all let go. Both Longfield and Lizzie had mentioned wanting to move to California.

Meanwhile, the president of the bank in Hamburg sent a reply telegram to Johnson & Company undertakers, stating that "neither Allen nor myself know of the relatives of Mrs. Bernard. Her husband [is] supposed to be in Wichita, Kansas."

In putting the pieces together, the newspaper reported that, "The story of Joseph E. Jones, that he traveled with the couple from Denver, and that they quarreled, with the result that the man deserted the girl at Orange, is doubtless correct. The girl invented the story of her brother to account for her presence at Coronado without money, baggage or friends."

~

SAN DIEGO UNION
Monday, December 5, 1892
Not Yet Claimed: Remains of the Coronado Suicide Still at the Morgue.

This short article brings San Diego readers up to date: no one has yet claimed Kate's body, although "many curious people dropped in yesterday to look at the dead girl, among them being a number of ladies." Meanwhile, the Hamburg, Iowa, bank president telegraphed that he thought Mrs. Lottie Bernard's husband was named John (a man he had never met). And, finally (still believing the body to be that of Lizzie Wyllie, alias Lottie Bernard), the news story reported, "A cousin of the suicide, who resides at Pasadena, was expected to arrive in the city on last night's train to identify the body. The mystery which has surrounded the case for the last week will probably be cleared today."

~

SAN DIEGO UNION
Tuesday, December 6, 1892
Further Evidence: Circumstances Tending to the Identification of the Suicide. Incidental Proof that the Wretched Girl was Miss Lizzie Wyllie of Detroit – No One Yet Here to Take Charge of the Remains.

"No one now believes that 'Mrs. Lottie A. Bernard,' the Coronado suicide, is other than pretty Lizzie Wyllie, daughter of Mrs. Elizabeth Wyllie of Detroit, who mysteriously disappeared from her home some six weeks ago ... all that yet remains to fully solve the mystery is the identification of the dead girl by some relative." Unfortunately, as the newspaper points out, a relative – due in from Pasadena – "has not yet materialized."

Meanwhile, the "Bernard" connection was still being pursued (even though that name was thought to have been an alias). In the process, a Mr. John Bernard, from Wichita, Kansas, had been notified (again, via telegraph) that his wife "had suicided," but Bernard "had not seen fit to make any inquiries concerning his better half."

More details are also added to the Lizzie love story: "John G. Longfield ... was the foreman. He was so attentive to Lizzie that both he and the girl were discharged. They still continued to go together, notwithstanding that Lizzie knew he was married."

And to thicken the plot: "After her discharge, Lizzie made a long visit to her married sister, Mrs. Anderson, in Grand Rapids, and returned to her home a little over six weeks ago. This accounts for the girl's having several handkerchiefs among her effects marked 'Lottie Anderson.' "

Although Lizzie's mother believed that the dead girl was her daughter (just like the corpse, Lizzie had two moles on her cheek), questions still remained. "The family can solve the Hamburg part of the tragedy in no way, except that Longfield was at Hamburg under an assumed name and sent Lizzie the $25. If this be the case, who came to California with her, with whom did she have a quarrel at Orange, and who was the man that left her at that point? Who was the dead girl expecting at Hotel del Coronado? Not a brother, but one Longfield. If the truth were known, Allen of Hamburg may have played a leading part in the dastardly affair himself. Longfield is known at Detroit as a sport, and a rounder of not the best reputation even for one of his class."

Lizzie, meanwhile, was at the morgue, her face "natural and as peaceful as though she were asleep at home." Authorities were still awaiting instructions from Mrs. Wyllie on what to do with the body, and the three trunks at the railroad depot were yet unclaimed.

~

SAN DIEGO UNION
Wednesday, December 7, 1892
Not Yet Fully Determined: The Coronado Suicide's Identity Still a Matter of Conjecture.

Two days previously, in hopes of identifying the dead girl once and for all, the undertaker sent a photograph of her face to Mrs. Wyllie in Detroit, and he did note at least one physical discrepancy: Lizzie had pierced ears, and the dead girl didn't. In addition, the handkerchiefs found among Kate's possessions were reexamined and found to be embroidered not with "Lottie Anderson," but with the name "Louisa Anderson." As a result, it was decided that Lizzie's aunt, Mrs. Anderson of Grand Rapids, Michigan, would be questioned about her given name: "If it is Louisa instead of Lottie, the last doubt will be removed as to the dead girl's identity."

Meanwhile, this same article relayed a dispatch from Hamburg, Iowa, dated December 6 (the day before): "It is not believed here that Mrs. L. Anderson Bernard, who killed herself at Coronado, was Lizzie Wyllie of Detroit. It has been learned that there was recently in this place a man named L.A. Bernard, a professional gambler, and he is believed to have been the suicide's husband. Bernard left Hamburg November 7 for Topeka. He said his wife was sick in California and he intended to bring her back to Iowa. He tried to borrow money for that purpose, but failed. No word has since been received from him. G.L. Allen of this place, to whom the woman telegraphed for money, was a schoolmate of Bernard's in Illinois, and had never met Mrs. Bernard. Simply out of charity he sent her $25. Therefore it is strongly believed here that the Detroit identification [as Lizzie Wyllie] is a mistake."

But the San Diego newspaper disagreed with the contents of the dispatch: "The story is not believed in San Diego. On the contrary, it strengthens the opinion that somehow Allen is more deeply interested than to the extent of $25, and has invented the above as a blind. A San Diego man, who happens to know Allen, says he is a cattleman, of some wealth, a sport and a lady killer. The situation in this mysterious case resolves itself to this – either Allen is a consummate liar and had dealings with Lizzie Wyllie, which he is trying to conceal, or the girl lying on a slab at the morgue here is Mrs. L.A. Bernard, the wife of a gambler."

~

SAN DIEGO UNION
Thursday, December 8, 1892

Darker Than Ever: The Mysterious Suicide is Not Lizzie Wyllie of Detroit. Lizzie's Ears are Pierced, and the Dead Girl's are Not – A Possible Clue from Orange, where the Pretty Stranger Stopped.

Based on the fact that Lizzie Wyllie had pierced ears and wore silver earrings – and the dead girl did not – it was ultimately determined that the corpse was definitely not Lizzie Wyllie.

"The mystery, therefore, becomes as dark as ever, unless the story of G.L. Allen of Hamburg, Iowa, is accepted which is to the effect that he was a schoolmate of a gambler named Bernard, whose wife was sick in California, and that, upon her telegraphed request, he sent her $25 for charity's sake, never having seen her. There are several points in his story, however, which are open to question. If Bernard was at Hamburg and tried to raise the money to bring his sick wife east, why did not Allen lend him the money then? It is strongly believed that if the suicide is really Mrs. Bernard, there was a cause for Allen's promptness in remitting the money to her in some pull or influence that Allen did not wish to become known. Allen has delayed and equivocated in the matter, if not actually lying, in a manner strongly suspicious. Telegrams to him and to the city marshal of Hamburg, asking for information are still unanswered."

In the meantime, another possible identity was put forth by Miss Florence S. Howard, writing from Orange, California. In this case, Kate is identified as Josie Brown, 24 years old, and from Detroit, who had stayed with Miss Howard the previous summer (although the writer did not speculate about why Josie Brown would have registered at the hotel under an assumed name). Miss Howard's telegram concludes, "She said her sister's name was Mrs. Anderson. There was a young man here part of the time who said he was Miss Brown's brother, Dr. Brown of Detroit, although he had been in Minneapolis."

The newspaper summed up the mystery this way: "There is nothing to indicate that this may not be the dead person, and that she is really Mrs. Bernard. Steps have been taken to learn the connection of Allen with the case, as thus far, since the girl is not Lizzie Wyllie, that is the only clue upon which to work."

And, finally, regarding the unclaimed trunks (that may or may not have been Kate's), "Another attempt will be made today to open the three trunks left uncalled for at the D Street depot, in view of the fact that the mysterious woman's identity is again in the dark."

~

SAN DIEGO UNION
Friday, December 9, 1892
The Gambler's Wife: Her Life in Los Angeles Previous to Suicide.

"The girl who committed suicide at Hotel del Coronado has made lots of trouble by burning her letters and papers. She has been almost positively identified twice, and her personality is again in doubt. She is not Lizzie Wyllie, who is living with the paramour Longfield in Ontario, Canada. The question is, is she Mrs. Bernard? Little doubt exists that she is the wife of the Iowa gambler."

To further complicate matters, the Los Angeles chief of police had notified San Diego's police chief to let him know that the suicide victim was probably Mrs. Kate Logan of Los Angeles. Apparently, Kate Logan had disappeared the day before Thanksgiving.

According to the newspaper, "The matter all indicates that Mrs. Bernard is really the woman's name, that she was at Orange last year under the name of Josie Brown; that she was at Omaha two months ago, where she perhaps met Allen of Hamburg; that she came to Los Angeles under the name of Kate Morgan, and thence appeared here under her real name. There is still much mystery in the case, as for instance her connection with Allen, the unknown man at Orange, and the final reasons for her suicide."

~

SAN DIEGO UNION
Saturday, December 10, 1892

No Longer a Mystery: Identity of the Coronado Suicide Clearly Established. Bernard an Assumed Name – Married to a Gambler at Hamburg, Iowa – a Domestic at Los Angeles – Box Marked "Louisa Anderson."

"The trunk of Mrs. Kate Morgan, who has been missing from Los Angeles since November 23, was opened in that city Thursday, and the contents revealed beyond reasonable doubt that Kate Morgan and 'Mrs. L.A. Bernard,' who committed suicide at Coronado, are the same person." [This trunk was one Kate had left behind at her employer's house in Los Angeles, not to be confused with the unclaimed trunks still waiting to be identified at the San Diego train station.]

"A tin box was found marked 'Louisa Anderson,' which is the same name as that marked on the suicide's handkerchiefs. Photographs and a lock of hair were found. The photograph of Mrs. Morgan was among the lot, and the Los Angeles Herald says that the picture does not resemble the description of the Coronado suicide. Yet other evidence is too strong to admit of doubt as to the identification. A marriage certificate was found setting forth that Thomas E. Morgan and Kate K. Farmer were united at Hamburg, Iowa, on December 30, 1885, by Reverend W.E. Howe. From data found, the history of the unfortunate woman will soon be learned."

The article reported that Kate had been a domestic in Los Angeles in the employ of L.A. Grant. "She was very reticent concerning her past life, merely saying that she had married a gambler and was not happy with him."

Quoted from a *Los Angeles Times* report, the *San Diego Union* added that Kate had only been in California a few months, previously working for a W.T. Farmer, possibly a relative, in Hanford, California. Police claimed Kate traveled from Chicago to Omaha, to Cheyenne, to Ogden, to Sacramento, to Hanford (where she picked up a letter of recommendation from Mr. Farmer) and finally to Los Angeles.

"From the condition of the papers, photographs, etc., in her trunk, she was desirous of concealing her identity, as every name, date and address, except the marriage certificate, had been destroyed."

"A telegram was sent to Mr. Farmer at Hanford, and his answer is awaited for instructions as to the disposal of the body. The connection of G.L. Allen, of Hamburg, with the case is still a mystery. He knew that the name 'Bernard' was assumed, as the gambler husband was at Hamburg a month ago under the same name, and Allen said he was an old schoolmate."

The article concluded, "In all probability, the unfortunate woman will be buried here."

~

SAN DIEGO UNION
Sunday, December 11, 1892
The Facts Unfolding: Further Information as to the Identity of the Coronado Suicide.

The day before, the following letter had been received by the coroner from A.D. Swarts of Los Angeles: "I see by this morning's Times that the suicide at Coronado hotel is Mrs. Kate or Tom Morgan. If this is true, I have known her ever since '69. Joe Chandler of Riverton (a miller) is her grandfather, and I think if informed of her death would see that she has a decent burial. Tom Morgan, Sr., her husband's uncle, lives near Hamburg, Iowa, and is quite wealthy. Her husband has a number of rich relatives."

As a result of this telegram, "telegrams were accordingly sent to the parties named, asking for instructions for disposing of the body."

As a sidelight, the newspaper also reported that "the number of visitors at Johnson's undertaking parlors to view the girl is as large as ever. The visitors are mostly ladies."

And, finally, "The three trunks at the D Street depot supposed to have belonged to the girl have been claimed by the owners. No doubt now remains but that the suicide is Mrs. Kate Morgan."

~

SAN DIEGO UNION
Monday, December 12, 1892
He Owns Her: The Grandfather of the Unfortunate Suicide Will Bury Her.

Kate's grandfather – in an incredibly terse telegram from Riverton, Iowa – informed the undertaker that "Your telegram received regarding Kate Morgan, nee Farmer." Kate's grandfather went on to instruct the undertaker to "Bury her and send me statement," and was signed "J.W. Chandler."

The newspaper explained, "Mr. Chandler is the wealthy grandfather of the unfortunate girl. None of her other relatives have uttered a word, and there is still a mystery as to the cause of her suicide. She will be buried today, just two weeks after she put a bullet in her brain."

~

SAN DIEGO UNION
Wednesday, December 14, 1892
Buried at Mount Hope.

"The funeral of Mrs. Kate Morgan, the unfortunate woman who committed suicide some two weeks ago at the Hotel del Coronado, took place yesterday morning at 10 o'clock at the parlors of Johnson & Company, undertakers. The Reverend H.B. Restarick officiated, reading some passages of scripture and offering prayers. Several members of the Brotherhood of St. Andrew were present, and these with some ladies of the Episcopal church present made responses when they occurred in the service. Quite a number of persons were present. At the close of the service the casket was placed in the hearse for conveyance to Mount Hope Cemetery, where the body was interred."

~

And so ends the *San Diego Union*'s coverage of Kate's mysterious suicide; however, there were other newspapers in California – even in San Diego – that published their own versions of Kate's story. Additional excerpts are included in the next chapter.

Kate Morgan checked into the hotel on November 24, 1892. Five days later she was found dead on an exterior hotel staircase.

HOTEL DEL CORONADO,

E. S. BABCOCK, Manager. **Coronado, California.**

Money, Jewels, and other valuable Packages, must be placed in the Safe in the office, otherwise the Proprietors will not be responsible for any loss.

27070 C

NAMES.	RESIDENCE.	ROOMS.	TIME.
Thursday Nov. 24th 1892			
Mark J. Williams	N.Y. City	302	L.
Henry Perrin	Pawtucket R.I.	151	"
Miss R. A. Gage	Pawtucket R.I.	153	"
Mrs M. E. French	Pawtucket R.I.	153	"
Geo Nester	Detroit M.	113	"
Mrs R. Irwin	Denver Colo	315	"
Grace Irwin	Denver Colo	315	"
Miss Lottie A Bernard	Detroit	302	D
Jos A Jones	Boston	371	"
W A Clark + wife	Coronado	chgd	"
Fran E Clark	"	"	"
H C Moore	New Mex	196	S.

When Kate Morgan registered as "Miss Lottie A. Bernard," a desk clerk signed her in.

Drawing of Kate Morgan by KL, who encountered The Del's famous ghost almost 100 years after Kate died.
KL's story is on page 92.

At the inquest, one of the witnesses testified that he had seen Kate Morgan for the last time on an oceanfront veranda.

CERTIFICATE OF DEATH. ✓ 188

CORONER'S OFFICE,
CITY AND COUNTY OF SAN DIEGO.

San Diego, Cal., Dec 12 1892.

Name Mrs Kate Morgan

Aged 24 *years,* ~~*Male.*~~ *Female.*

Occupation —— *Married.* ~~*Single. Widow. Widower.*~~

Place of Birth State or Country Iowa *Nationality* American

How long resident of this City or County, 4 days *years.*

Previous Residence, Los Angeles *Race* White

Place of Death, Coronado Beach

Date of Death, November 29th 1892

Date of Burial, December 13th 1892

Place of Interment, Mt Hope *Cemetery.*

Johnson & Co *Undertaker.*

CORONER'S CERTIFICATE.

I, M. B. Kellar *Coroner, do hereby Certify, that having made all needed examination and inquiries on the body of above described decedent, I do hereby certify, that* Mrs Kate *came to* her *death in this* County *by* a pistol shot inflicted by her own hand with suicidal intent

M. B. Kellar.
Coroner, City and County San Diego.
By H J Stetson Deputy Coroner

Although the Coroner's inquest listed Kate Morgan's date of death as November 28, 1892, her death certificate (above) records the date as November 29, 1892.

Kate Morgan was buried at Mount Hope Cemetery in San Diego; her gravesite draws hundreds of visitors every year.

Numerous guests and Del employees have witnessed the mystery of Kate Morgan firsthand, reporting that they've seen her ghost at various locations throughout the hotel.

Chapter 5

More Details Revealed:

Other San Diego and California Newspapers Cover the Coronado Mystery

The following selected excerpts provide additional information about Kate's life and death, or they report already established information in a new way. The articles below are organized by newspaper and then arranged chronologically under each newspaper's name.

~

THE DAILY BEE, SAN DIEGO
Tuesday, November 29, 1892
Blew Out Her Brains. Suicide of a Beautiful Young Woman at San Diego. Disappointed Over Not Receiving Money. After Her Death Word Came That She Could Draw All She Desired – She Was Well Dressed and Had a Good Sum in Her Purse.

"Between the thunderous surf of the gray sea and the brilliancy and music of a gay throng in the great parlor and the long halls of the Hotel del Coronado, a woman stood last night alone and desperate. From her position on the stone stairs at the west end of the ocean terrace leading to the beach [this is one of the few instances where the location of Kate's body was accurately given], the surf wrapped and re-wrapped her with its spray, and the pitiless rain fell upon her bared head and young white face."

"Whatever it may have been, fear or courage at the final moment, there is no one to say."

"All that is known of the stranger is that she arrived with no luggage but a hand satchel on the 24th and gave her name as Mrs. L. Anderson Bernard, of Detroit. She remained in her room generally and seemed to suffer intensely."

~

THE DAILY BEE, SAN DIEGO
Thursday, December 1, 1892
Why She Died. The Woman Who Suicided at San Diego Had Been Wronged.

"It is now thought that the woman registered at the Hotel Coronado as Lottie Anderson Bernard, who committed suicide Tuesday, was not suffering from cancer in her stomach, but had been ruined, and realizing that she had been deserted as well, decided to end her troubles."

"She was a beautiful woman, and when arriving here on Thanksgiving Day did not appear ill or unhappy. Her evident anxiety to trace the whereabouts of Anderson [the man Kate identified as her brother] and her distress on receiving no advices from him after going to the Hotel del Coronado, are now believed to prove that the man was not her brother, but one who was responsible for her condition."

~

THE DAILY BEE, SAN DIEGO
Tuesday, December 13, 1892

The Last Rites. Burial of the Woman Who Suicided at San Diego.

"There were many women in attendance. Prominent ladies sent flowers for the casket, but no one followed the remains to the cemetery."

~

THE SEAPORT NEWS, SAN DIEGO
Saturday, December 3, 1892

Weary of Life.

"Mrs. Anderson Bernard, a widow [which Kate was not], twenty-four years of age, arrived at Del Coronado alone last week. She was reserved and mingling not with the other guests, made few acquaintances. It was known, however, that she was an invalid. On Monday she resolved to end her sorrows and sufferings, so crossing the bay purchased a revolver and cartridges."

"Soon after dark on that evening, she deserted the warm, cheerful rooms of the hotel for the darkness outside, and on the steps at the rear in the cold, drizzling rain, took her own life."

~

THE SEAPORT NEWS, SAN DIEGO
Saturday, December 10, 1892

Her Identity Established.

"The following from the Los Angeles Times settles the whole mystery in regard to the young lady who killed herself last week. It says: 'The trunk left at Contractor Grant's [the Los Angeles home in which Kate had been employed] by the woman who suicided at Coronado was opened yesterday, and from a marriage certificate found therein, it is certain that Hamburg, Iowa, was her home. She was married to Thomas E. Morgan by Rev. W.E. Howes, in December 1885. Her maiden name was Miss Katie E. Farmer. From the condition of her trunk she was evidently desirous of concealing her identity [this statement was not further explained]. Mr. Grant, where she lived in Los Angeles, says she started for San Diego on the 23rd of last month. She told other servants that she had married a gambler and was not happy with him.'"

~

LOS ANGELES TIMES
Thursday, December 1, 1892
Ended Her Troubles. Suicide of a Young Lady at the Hotel del Coronado.

"Her evident illness is attributed to medicines taken with the purpose of effecting a miscarriage, though this has not been fully demonstrated, no post-mortem examination having been authorized."

~

LOS ANGELES TIMES
Thursday, December 8, 1892
A Mystery Solved. Identity of Coronado Suicide Established. She Was Known as Mrs. Katie Logan [the alias Kate Morgan had used in Los Angeles] *in Los Angeles, Where She Worked as a Domestic in Several Families. Said to Have Been the Wife of a Gambler, Who Had Deserted Her – Her Departure for San Diego on the 23rd of November.*

"It has been left to Los Angeles to unravel the dark mystery surrounding the suicide of the unknown girl at the Coronado Hotel. Everything points to the fact that she lived in this city, where she was known as Mrs. Katie Logan, and she left here for San Diego the day before Thanksgiving, and had no baggage except her little gripsack and the shawl that has been written about so much."

"The young woman's trunk and baggage are now at Mrs. Grant's No. 917 South Hill Street, where she was last seen. When she left, on the 23rd, ult. [of the last month], she stated that she would be back in time for Thanksgiving dinner, but not a word has been heard from her since."

"Mrs. Logan came here from Omaha about two months ago, and stated that her parents lived near that place. She stated that her husband was a gambler, but she did not know what had become of him."

"She visited several employment agencies and first secured work as a domestic in R.M. Widney's house and from there she went to work for T.H. Hughes. Shortly before she disappeared she got employment at Mrs. Grant's, No. 917 South Hill Street."

"The day before she left this city, she was anxious to get some papers signed, and seemed to be greatly worried about something, but what it was no one seems to know."

"She wore the same ring as described in the dispatches, and the black underclothes are the same. Not only that, but Mrs. Logan had two moles on the left side of her face, and the unfortunate suicide at Coronado answers the description in every way. She also told several persons in this city that her name was Lizzie, but that she liked the name of Kittie better, and that was the reason she adopted it."

"It is believed that she came to Los Angeles from San Francisco, where she probably worked awhile after she reached the Coast. At any rate, she was well posted in San Francisco and knew all about the hotels and public places, showing that she must have lived there."

"The San Diego authorities were considerably puzzled over the young woman's knowledge of the streets and public buildings of Los Angeles and San Francisco [it is not clear how the newspapers found out about Kate's familiarity with Los Angeles and San Francisco], but it is plain now, for she certainly worked here and she must have lived in San Francisco."

"While in this city, Mrs. Logan bore an excellent reputation. She attended strictly to her duties all the time and was never out at night, and so far as is known, she did not have any men around her the whole time she was here."

"Even on the day of her departure for San Diego, she seemed to be in fairly good spirits, and promised faithfully that she would be home next day in time to cook the Thanksgiving dinner."

"The mystery that now surrounds the case is the paper she wanted to get signed or sworn to the day before she left. If that paper could be found the whole mystery would be cleared up."

"From her conversation, she was fairly well educated, and as her husband was a gambler she has done considerable traveling and has spent considerable of her life in the best hotels, which accounts for the fact that she was so much at home in the swell hotels in San Diego."

~

LOS ANGELES TIMES
Friday, December 9, 1892

The Coronado Suicide. Additional Evidence That it Was Mrs. Kate Morgan. Her Trunk Removed to the Police Station – Efforts to Conceal her Identity – What Mr. Grant Says About the Woman.

"The trunk left by Mrs. Kate Morgan, the young woman who met with such a tragic death at her own hands at the Coronado Hotel, at Contractor Grant's, where she worked, was removed to the central police station by order of Chief Glass yesterday."

"On opening the trunk, further evidence than that given by The Times yesterday, of her identity, was found."

"It will be remembered that just before the unfortunate girl took her life by her own hand, she telegraphed to a gentleman in Hamburg, Iowa, for money, and the authorities believed that she was related to him and he was notified of her death, simply stating that he knew her husband, who was a gambler and that he wired her $25 out of sympathy. For some reason he denied that he knew anything further about the case."

"From a marriage certificate found among her effects, it is certain that Hamburg was her home. She was married in that place to Thomas E. Morgan by Rev. W.E. Howes, on the 30th of December, 1885, and her maiden name was Miss Katie K. Farmer."

"Chief Glass telegraphed the chief of police of San Diego asking if the body had been identified and buried, or shipped off. The San Diego officer replied that the body is still unclaimed in Johnson's undertaking rooms."

"Mr. Grant was seen by a Times reporter yesterday afternoon, and stated that he and his family are positive that Katie Morgan and the San Diego suicide are one and the same person."

"He knows that she started for San Diego on the 23rd of last month, and the dead girl corresponds in every way with his former servant."

"None of the other servants about the house could induce Katie to talk about her past life to any great extent. She told them that she married a gambler and that she was not happy with him. Mr. Grant never had a better servant in his house, and when she failed to return on Thanksgiving day as she promised, Mr. Grant at once reported the matter to the police, and detectives have been working on it ever since."

"There has been considerable mystery surrounding the telegraphic report that the young woman possessed $1,600 when she committed suicide. This report grew out of a common mistake in telegraphic figures. The Coroner at San Diego found $16 on her person, and the sum was raised to $1,600 in the dispatches."

~

LOS ANGELES TIMES
Date Uncertain

The Coronado Suicide. Her Identity as Kate Morgan Established Beyond a Doubt.

"It will be in order for the detectives to ascertain what became of the young woman's money, if it is true, as stated by Mr. Farmer of Hanford that she had quite a sum when she left him to come to Los Angeles [W.T. Farmer, the relative Kate worked for, as referenced in the Saturday, December 10, 1892, *San Diego Union* article]. She told him that she intended to deposit it in a bank, and as she had employment all the time she was in this city, and was not extravagant, she could not have spent the money."

"If the detectives ascertain what disposition was made of the money, they are sure to get to the bottom of the cause of her suicide."

~

LOS ANGELES TIMES
Wednesday, December 14, 1892
The Coronado Suicide. Her Identity as Katie Morgan Fully Established – Farmer's Letter.

"It will be remembered that when The Times made public the identity of the mysterious Coronado Hotel suicide, while the detectives and other newspapers were floundering around in the dark, Chief Glass telegraphed Mr. Farmer, as he gave the unfortunate girl a letter of recommendation, but as Mr. Farmer lived out in the country, the dispatch had to be forwarded to him through the mails, hence the delay for almost a week."

"The gentleman's letter [Mr. Farmer's letter] reads as follows: 'Dear Sir [Chief Glass]: Your message received yesterday. I am more than surprised to hear of the tragedy. If it was Kate Morgan you can rest assured that it was no case of suicide, for the reason that she had no cause for committing such an act. When she left me I told her if she needed anything to send to me, and I would assist her. Her people are well-to-do. Her husband, Thomas Morgan, has been traveling in the interest of some manufacturing company. His home is Hamburg, Iowa. I have known them for a good many years. She wrote me soon after her arrival in Los Angeles that she had secured a situation at Mr. Whitney's, a banker, on the West Side. She had when she left here quite a sum of money, one large flat-top trunk, two leather satchels, and a lady's gold watch. She said she was going to deposit her money in a national bank for safekeeping.'"

"'Her relatives are Henry Broomback and Thomas Morgan, Hamburg, Iowa; Joe W. Chandler, her grandfather, and John Samuella, Riverton, Iowa. I cannot help but think there is some mistake about its being Kate Morgan. She was troubled with rheumatism while here, and went to Los Angeles on account of its fine climate, with intention of living there if she liked it. You say you have positive evidence that it is her. What is it? She has a second cousin living in this county. She certainly would have written to someone if she contemplated the awful act.'"

"There is no doubt about the identity of the unfortunate girl. She answered the description of the Coronado suicide in every particular. That Katie Morgan intended to commit suicide when she left her employer, Mr. Grant of this city, on the 23rd of last month, there is no doubt, for she did everything in her power to conceal her identity."

"There are several mysteries surrounding the case that may never be cleared up. If, as Mr. Farmer says, she had money when she left him, no one knows what became of it. The day before she left this city she drew up or had signed some kind of a legal paper, but the persons with whom she did business are not known, and for some reason they prefer to remain in the background. If she had money she must have disposed of it in some manner on that day, and at her request the matter is probably being kept a secret. The cause of her rash act is also a mystery."

"That her family in Hamburg, Iowa, are satisfied with the identity there can be no doubt, for the body was buried in San Diego at their expense last Saturday."

~

LOS ANGELES HERALD
Sunday, December 4, 1892

A Mystery Cleared Up. The Coronado Girl Suicide Identified. She was Miss Lizzie Wyllie [it turned out, of course, that the dead woman was not Lizzie Wyllie] *of Detroit. From Which Place She Eloped With a Married Man. She Was Undoubtedly Betrayed and Deserted – The Whereabouts of the Author of Her Ruin is Not Known.*

[From Detroit] "When Mrs. Wyllie saw the dispatches about the suicide of Lottie Anderson Bernard at San Diego, she telegraphed for a description of the dead girl. It came as follows, 'Height, five and a-half feet; complexion fair but sallow; medium length of black hair; two small moles on left cheek; broad features; high cheek bones; brown eyes; weight 150 pounds; age about 26; good teeth; plain gold ring on third finger of left hand; ring of pure gold, with four pearls and blue stone in center; black corsets; large black hat.'"

"This was an exact description of Lizzie. She [Mrs. Wyllie] at once telegraphed to her niece at Pasadena, California, who knew Lizzie, to go and see the body."

"The family cannot account for the $1,600 said to have been found on the body [this was a misprint; the amount was $16, not $1,600], nor her connection with the Hamburg, Iowa, bank. She [Lizzie Wyllie] was positively penniless when she left here [Detroit]."

~

LOS ANGELES HERALD
Friday, December 9, 1892

Not the Coronado Woman. But Plenty of Mystery About Mrs. Morgan. The Contents of Her Trunk Throw No Light on the Matter. Her Photograph Shows that She Did not Resemble the Coronado Hotel Suicide – Her Marriage Certificate – Other Details.

"A trunk marked 'Mrs. Kate Morgan' was taken to the central police station on yesterday from the house of L.A. Grant, 917 South Hill Street. Mr. Grant stated that Mrs. Morgan had been employed in his house as a domestic and that on the evening of November 23rd she left, stating that she would return on the next day. She took only a satchel, leaving her trunk of clothing. She did not return. The sudden disappearance was reported at the central police station but no clue was found of the missing woman."

"In her trunk was found a tin box marked 'Louise Anderson' [although this name was probably Louisa (as had been reported in other newspaper articles) and not Louise, this may have been still another Kate Morgan alias]. In the box were several photographs. One was that of a man aged about 50 years, with a full beard, tinged with gray; another was of a man aged about 35 years, black mustache, black hair, thick skull, and who looked something like a sporting character. This is perhaps the picture of her husband, who had deserted her. There were also photographs of two boys, aged about 9 and 10 years; the photograph of a girl of about 2 years; and still another of a babe."

"In a paper was a lock of pretty blonde hair. On the paper was written, in rather coarse characters, 'Elizabeth A. Morgan's hair.' On the reverse side of the photograph of the old gentleman, the name was scratched off but the written word 'Visalia' was left. On two other photographs the names had been carefully erased."

"A letter was found in the box recommending Mrs. Morgan as an honorable and trustworthy woman and signed by W.J. Farmer, Hanford, California. The photograph of the old gentleman is no doubt that of Farmer, and he is perhaps her uncle."

"There were also found the cards of several ladies, together with their addresses, where no doubt she had been sent for work. These were Mrs. J.H. McDonough, San Rafael; Mrs. M.R. Abbott, Fifth and Mission, San Francisco; Mrs. Ottinger, 602 Stock Exchange, San Francisco."

"A cabinet size photograph of Mrs. Morgan, found among the others, shows her to be a woman of about 26 years of age, black eyes, large ears, rather large, open face, and somewhat coarse features; her mouth is rather large and lips thick. The photograph contained not marks, and had evidently been taken recently. The photograph does not denote the appearance of a woman accustomed to stopping at first-class hotels as a guest, or one who wears lace shawls; neither does it show her to be pretty, and the features certainly are not those of a highly educated woman."

~

LOS ANGELES HERALD
Tuesday, December 13, 1892

The Coronado Suicide. Her Identity Seems to Be Well Established.

"Mr. Chandler is the wealthy grandfather of the unfortunate girl. None of her other relatives have uttered a word, and there is still a mystery as to the cause of her suicide. She was buried Saturday, just two weeks after she put a bullet in her brain."

~

THE EVENING EXPRESS, LOS ANGELES
Thursday, December 8, 1892

Is She the Woman? The Strange Suicide at the Coronado Still a Mystery.

"On Thanksgiving day, L.A. Grant, who resides at 917 South Hill Street, reported at police headquarters that a young woman named Mrs. Katie Morgan [although Grant knew her as Katie Logan], a domestic in the Grant household, was missing. The woman, whose former husband was a gambler, was described as being very pretty. When she disappeared she left all her worldly possessions at Mr. Grant's house."

~

SAN FRANCISCO CHRONICLE
Thursday, December 1, 1892

Coronado's Puzzle. Peculiar Actions of Miss Barnard [Kate's alias was misspelled here]. *New Facts Developed at the Inquest. Theories That a Man is Indirectly Concerned in the Suicide Case.*

"The inquest upon the remains of the woman who committed suicide at the ocean's edge at Coronado beach on Monday night, was held today and resulted in a verdict of suicide. The verdict was undoubtedly correct, but fails utterly to give satisfaction to the public mind since the identity of the woman is not positively fixed, and the cause of the suicide is left enveloped in mystery. Public opinion is to the effect that the contradictory stories told by the victim of her own unwillingness to face the world were not true, and that a man is connected with the story somewhere."

"She left the Coronado [hotel] at noon on Monday [to go into San Diego]. She asked the conductor where she could find a hardware store and was directed to one. The conductor had to lift her off the car, as she was very weak. Her walk and nervous manner attracted attention."

"It appears to be the general opinion that however ill Miss Bernard may have been, she had some great trouble weighing on her mind during the time she was at the hotel."

"When arriving at San Diego on Monday her excuse given at the hotel [as the reason for traveling over to San Diego] was that she must come personally to identify her trunks, there being no checks, and yet on reaching this side of the bay she made no outcry about her baggage, but departed to purchase a revolver, with which she ended her existence."

"A physician who has seen the body gives voice to the opinion that the woman was not suffering from cancer of the stomach. No baggage is in the city that can be identified as hers, and more light on the matter is anxiously awaited."

~

SAN FRANCISCO CHRONICLE
Friday, December 2, 1892
Still Unknown. No Clue to the Identity of the Coronado Suicide.

"Thus far there is no clue to the identity of Lottie Anderson Bernard, the Coronado suicide. The Iowa man who responded to her appeal for money [G.L. Allen of Hamburg, Iowa, who sent $25 to the hotel] has shut up like a clam and refuses to answer telegrams, though several have been sent to him."

"No report can be secured as to Doctor Anderson of Minneapolis [the man Kate identified as her brother] and none know whether or not he is a myth. One fact was brought to light today, however, by the report that Joseph E. Jones of Boston, who arrived at Coronado on Thanksgiving day, came across the continent on the same train with the young woman and asserts that she was accompanied by a man at least from as far east as Denver. The two, Mr. Jones says, quarreled on the train, and after reaching California their quarrel became marked. Loud words were used, and the woman seemed to be beseeching her escort, whether husband, brother or lover, to forgive her. This man, Mr. Jones says, left the train at some station north of here."

~

SAN FRANCISCO CHRONICLE
Sunday, December 4, 1892

Her Name Was Wyllie. Identity of the Coronado Suicide. She Eloped With a Married Man. The Dead Girl Was a Bookbinder of Detroit and Was Out of Employment.

"Driven almost to distraction by worry and shame, Mrs. Elizabeth Wyllie of Detroit admitted this afternoon that it was her daughter Lizzie who was found dead with a bullet wound in her head, inflicted by her own hand, on the sands of the ocean beach at San Diego, California, last Tuesday night. With the stricken mother's admission came the statement that her daughter had eloped a month before with a married man of this city. The young woman left here without a dollar and her paramour was known to have but little money."

"Five weeks ago last Monday she [Lizzie] went out ostensibly to go downtown on an errand. She never returned. It soon became evident to the girl's relatives that her errand was not to secure work and that she did not go alone. By a little investigation they discovered that a Detroit man, whom they suspected, had also disappeared. He had been calling on Lizzie occasionally, but was regarded by the family merely as a friend, not as a lover."

"On the Saturday before Lizzie's disappearance this man called in the afternoon at the Wyllie house and bade all of them goodbye. He said he was going south and would probably reach Southern California before he returned. 'I will be picking roses in California while your feet are freezing in Detroit,' he said to May Wyllie, jocosely."

"The dispatches described Mrs. Bernard as of prepossessing appearance, and Lizzie was certainly an attractive girl. The name 'L. Anderson Bernard' was suggestive of the lost daughter. The initial is that of the name of Lizzie and Anderson is the name of her married sister in Grand Rapids."

"Mrs. Wyllie read the telegram [describing the dead girl] as far as the mention of the two moles and then the paper dropped from her hands. 'My Lizzie; it's my Lizzie,' she sobbed repeatedly. 'What will become of me?' Not a word of reproach came from her lips upon the name of the dead girl."

"John G. Longfield, a local bookbinder under whom Lizzie worked, is the man with whom she eloped. He is married, and left behind a wife and two children. Mrs. Longfield, while admitting that her husband has not been home for five weeks, says he has been at work in Cleveland all the time and is there now."

~

SAN FRANCISCO CHRONICLE
Tuesday, December 6, 1892

Her Name in Doubt. Mystery of the Coronado Suicide. The Detroit Identification Questioned. Many Reasons to Believe That the Woman Was Not Lizzie Wyllie. Points to be Explained. The Dead Woman Neither Acted Nor Spoke Like a Bindery Employee.

"The clerks at the Hotel del Coronado speak of the dead woman as better educated than the usual run of bookbindery girls and more refined than one who had been discharged for being intimate with a man would be. Furthermore, a bookbindery girl running away with a fellow-workman would hardly go to a fashionable place like the Hotel del Coronado. They would seek a hotel more suited to their class. She is said, also, to have spoken with more familiarity of the Palace in San Francisco and of the Westminster and Nadeau in Los Angeles than would be expected of a factory girl only a month from Detroit."

~

SAN FRANCISCO CHRONICLE
Tuesday, December 6, 1892
Longfield Heard From. A Letter From Miss Wyllie That May Clear Up the Case.

"Mrs. Longfield [the wife of John G. Longfield, the man who was suspected of accompanying Lizzie Wyllie to California] addressed a letter to her husband in Cleveland on Saturday. As she does not know his address she sent it to the general delivery. This morning she received the following dispatch from him in reply: 'I received a letter from Miss Wyllie last Wednesday. Will send it on at once. There is no truth in it.'"

~

SAN FRANCISCO CHRONICLE
Wednesday, December 7, 1892
Not Lizzie Wyllie. The Coronado Mystery About Solved. Mrs. Bernard, Who Committed Suicide, Was an Iowa Gambler's Wife.

"Miss Lizzie Wyllie of Detroit and Mrs. L. Anderson Bernard, who committed suicide at San Diego last week, were not the same persons. The Wyllie girl is alive and in Toronto and Mrs. Bernard is supposed to have been the wife of a Hamburg, Iowa, gambler. She had been in California for some time. G.L. Allen, who telegraphed her $25 on November 25th did so because he was a schoolmate of Bernard."

"As he promised in his dispatch of yesterday Longfield, whose name has been associated with Miss Wyllie's disappearance, enclosed to his wife a letter from Miss Wyllie, dated Toronto, in which she says that she is not coming home ... and indicates that Lizzie left home on account of trouble with her family."

~

SAN FRANCISCO CHRONICLE
Thursday, December 8, 1892
Wore No Earrings. The Coronado Suicide Still Unidentified. Both San Diego and Los Angeles Have New Theories to Fit the Case.

"It is believed that the unknown suicide at the Coronado Hotel was Mrs. Katie Logan, who worked as a domestic in several families in the city. Mrs. Logan came to this city from Omaha about two months ago. She said that her husband was a gambler, but that she did not know where he was. She left on November 23rd, promising to return on the following day, since which time nothing has been heard of her."

"The description fits her exactly. Her baggage is still at the place where she last worked, as when she left she only had a small satchel and a shawl. It is believed that Mrs. Logan also lived in San Francisco, as she was well informed about that city."

~

SAN FRANCISCO CHRONICLE
Friday, December 9, 1892
The Girl Suicide. Kate Morgan Probably Her Name. New Facts Which May Tend to Clear Away the Coronado Mystery.

"There appears to be little doubt that the girl who recently committed suicide at the Coronado Hotel in San Diego was Mrs. Kate Morgan, who worked for Contractor Grant, and left for San Diego the day before Thanksgiving."

"Mrs. Morgan came here from Omaha about two months ago and stated that her parents lived near that place and that her husband was a gambler, but she did not know what had become of him. She visited several employment agencies and first secured work as a domestic in R.M. Widney's residence, and from there she went to work for T.H. Hughes. Shortly before she disappeared she obtained employment at Mrs. Grant's, 917 South Hill Street."

"The day before she left this city she was anxious to get some papers signed, and seemed to be greatly worried about something, but what it was no one seemed to know. From a marriage certificate found among her effects, it is certain that Hamburg, Iowa, was her home."

"Her maiden name was Katie K. Farmer. She had only been on the coast a few months, and as near as can be learned, she worked for W.T. Farmer, a supposed relative, at Hanford, Tulare County."

"Mr. Grant was seen by a reporter this afternoon, and stated that he and his family were positive that Kate Morgan and the San Diego suicide were one and the same person. None of the other servants about the house could induce Katie to talk about her past life to any great extent. She told them that she had married a gambler and her marriage was not a happy one."

CHAPTER 6

Kate Morgan in San Diego:

Travel and Tribulation

Kate Morgan's Activities on the Day She Died

When Kate traveled into San Diego on November 28, 1892, she made her way to the 600 block of Fifth Street. In the 1890s, San Diego was much smaller than it is today, and the 600 block of Fifth Street would have been the center of downtown. Today, a larger metropolis surrounds the area, but this historic neighborhood is still considered the center of old San Diego. Preserved as the "Gaslamp Quarter," it features compact streets, turn-of-the-century buildings and lots of great restaurants and shops.

Directions to the Gaslamp Quarter:

To reach the Gaslamp Quarter from the Hotel del Coronado, take Orange Avenue to Fourth Street; turn right on Fourth Street, and proceed across the Coronado Bridge to Interstate 5 North. Follow Interstate 5 North to the Sixth Avenue exit. Turn left on Sixth Avenue and follow Sixth Avenue past Broadway to Market Street. Turn right on Market Street, then right on Fifth Avenue (you will be in the 600 block of Fifth Avenue).

Kate made the following stops on Fifth Avenue (in 1892, numbered avenues were called "streets"):

First Stop:
Ship Chandlery Store, 624 Fifth Street

This address no longer exists as a separate street number; however there is a restaurant at 622 Fifth Avenue and another restaurant at 628 Fifth Avenue.

Second Stop:
Chick's Gun Shop, 641 Fifth Street

Today, only 635 Fifth Avenue (a store) and 643 Fifth Avenue (a restaurant) exist as separate street numbers.

Third Stop:
Schiller & Murtha's (a men's store), 600-612 Fifth Street:

Today, 600 Fifth Avenue is a restaurant; there is no 612 Fifth Avenue.

~

Kate Morgan is Laid to Rest

After her death, Kate was taken to Johnson & Company (undertakers), 907 Sixth Street (the corner of Sixth Street and E Avenue). Today there is a store in this building.

One of the most interesting – though ghoulish – footnotes to the Kate Morgan story is the way in which her body was made available for widespread public viewing. In what seems to have been standard for the times, Kate's body was on display at Johnson & Company until she was positively identified or possibly even until she was buried. During that time, newspapers kept a running tally of the number of spectators who passed by (most of whom were women). And although some people (presumably unknown to Kate) sent flowers to the funeral parlor, no one accompanied Kate's body to Mount Hope Cemetery where she was buried.

Address for Mount Hope Cemetery:
3751 Market Street, San Diego (619-527-3400)
The cemetery is open from 8 a.m. to 4 p.m. daily, including holidays.

Directions to Mount Hope Cemetery:
To reach Mount Hope Cemetery from The Del, take Interstate 5 South to Interstate 15 North, exit right on Market Street. Proceed on Market Street for approximately one-half mile. As you pass Gateway Center Drive (on the left), you will begin to see the cemetery on the right. The cemetery entrance is on the right-hand side, just past Gateway Center Drive (the cemetery entrance is not well marked).

To reach Kate's gravesite, follow Horton Avenue into the cemetery and past the cemetery office (which is on the left). Continue following Horton Avenue. After crossing the railroad tracks, take an immediate left on Sessions Avenue. Follow Sessions Avenue past Grevilla Street. Sessions will intersect with Grevilla a second time near the gravesite. There is a small turn-out area where you can park and walk to the grave. Kate's gravesite is ahead (toward the railroad tracks below the hill) and slightly to the left. The grave is marked by a small white angel and a white vase (see photograph on page 59).

The official location of Kate's grave at Mount Hope Cemetery is: Lot 28, Row 6, Section 1, Division 5.

Chapter 7

Putting the Rumors to Rest:
Dispelling the Myths About Kate Morgan

Over the years, many intriguing stories have emerged about the life and death of Kate Morgan; however, many of these are not supported by the facts contained in the inquest or in newspaper articles. Although these two sources are admittedly flawed – both in scope and content – they do provide the basis for all we know about Kate Morgan.

Still, it is interesting to entertain alternative theories, even if they can't be substantiated.

Was Kate Murdered?
Although the coroner's inquest seems to leave little doubt that Kate died by her own hand, it has been suggested that she may have, in fact, been murdered. However, with witness after witness describing Kate's ill health, her despair and her exhausting trip into San Diego (to purchase a gun), it seems almost certain that Kate did, indeed, kill herself.

Certainly, 19th-century forensic science wasn't what it is today; still everything about Kate's behavior points to suicide. In addition, the community of San Diego had been captivated by Kate's story, and if there had been even the possibility of murder, the city would have been highly motivated to find the killer who had stilled the heart of its "Beautiful Stranger."

If Kate had been murdered, who was the murderer and what would the motive have been? The husband is always suspect, but in Kate's case, her husband may not have been anywhere near Southern California at the time of her death. Perhaps the man who deserted Kate in the city of Orange was not her husband, but her lover. If so, what reason might he have to kill Kate – when he could just as easily walk away from her? (Which is what he seems to have done.)

Was Kate Killed by Jumping – or Being Pushed – Off the Hotel's Turret?
This story always makes the rounds from time to time, but there is no truth to it.

Was Kate Pregnant?
It's not a far stretch to speculate that a young woman, estranged from her husband and pregnant (with her husband's child or even another man's child), might be the murder target for either man, but was Kate pregnant at the time of her death? This fact was never determined.

Considering the times in which she lived, if Kate had been pregnant (especially with another man's child), ending her own life may have seemed like her only alternative (a more likely scenario than being murdered). But perhaps Kate wasn't pregnant at all – just broken-hearted, in love with a man (her husband or another man) who had deserted her. This could have been reason enough – in Kate's mind – to take her own life.

Was Tom a Gambler?
Tom was identified matter-of-factly as "a gambler" in many of the newspaper articles, and this was also how Kate always described him to others.

Did Kate and Tom Morgan Pose as Siblings to Better Swindle Tom's Card-Playing Clientele?
Although it doesn't appear that Kate ever participated in gambling herself, the following myth persists: It has been said that Tom and Kate Morgan earned their living by riding the rails and gambling. Posing as brother and sister – so that Kate could flirtatiously distract Tom's male opponents – the two supposedly lived the high life from one corner of the continent to the other. This urban myth concludes with the following unsubstantiated postscript: In Tom's line of work, a pregnant partner was a liability, and he deserted Kate because she was pregnant.

Although this is a compelling tale, it is unlikely!

Was Kate's Violent Death Witnessed by a Hotel Maid?
Another Kate Morgan saga – with a life of its own – is the story that a hotel maid actually witnessed Kate's murder (or suicide) and then mysteriously disappeared, never to be seen or heard from again. While it is amazing that the hotel housekeeper who attended Kate was not interviewed during the inquest (nor did the newspapers ever seem to get a hold of her), there is nothing to support this story that sometimes circulates.

Like many other myths, this version of Kate's death is multilayered: because this maid supposedly witnessed Kate's death, the spirit of the unidentified housekeeper also haunts The Del – in Room 3519 (which, as the story goes, was the maid's room). Although Room 3519 has seen its share of supernatural activity (see Chapter 9 for more details), there is nothing to tie it to the Kate Morgan story, and no reason to believe that this room was ever even occupied by a maid, much less by the maid who attended Kate Morgan.

Chapter 8

The Hotel del Coronado in 1892:

What The Del Was Like at the Time of Kate Morgan's Visit

At the time of Kate Morgan's suicide, San Diego was a fairly small city (of about 16,000 people), having lost a lot of its population in 1888, when an economic depression began sweeping the country. Coronado, in turn, was just being developed, and was more "rural" than villagelike.

California, meanwhile, was like no other place in the world. Made rich – and famous – by the 1848 gold rush in Northern California, California became known around the world as the "golden state." Southern California, in turn, had its own pot of gold: endless sunshine. Considering all of California's native riches, it's not hard to imagine why Kate Morgan (and her husband) might have been drawn to the coast. An early Hotel Del brochure described Coronado as "a spot of earth where doctors have little employment, and where all the year is summer, and every day has genial sunshine, and gentle, balmy breezes."

Railroad companies had vigorously started promoting California, even before the first transcontinental rail line had been completed in 1869. So, by 1892 – the year of Kate's visit – the entire country was well aware that California was a wonderful place to live, work or play – and the best way to get there was by train.

In 1892, the Hotel del Coronado was brand-new, having received its first guests just four years earlier. Brand-new, but not yet bustling. The 1888 depression had taken its toll, and November was not part of the hotel's "season" (its busiest time), which would have been between December and April. Considering all this, it is very likely that the hotel was not very full during Thanksgiving week 1892. Perhaps this is the reason Kate's activities could be so well documented after her death.

Thanksgiving itself was not the holiday we celebrate today. Although President Lincoln had designated Thanksgiving a national holiday in 1863, it wasn't until the 1930s that most Americans began to celebrate Thanksgiving as a day off from work. And although Thanksgiving 1892 did fall on the fourth Thursday in November, it wasn't until 1941 that Congress established the fourth Thursday in November as the official Thanksgiving Day.

When Kate Morgan checked into the Hotel del Coronado, it's very likely that she entered through the "ladies' entrance." This was a courtesy offered by most Victorian hotels so that a single woman could check in discreetly. Today, only the main entrance remains (the ladies' entrance would have been to the left of the hotel's present entrance). The hotel also offered a separate dining room for unescorted women (apart from the Crown Room); this provided an alternative for women who were not comfortable dining in mixed company. Although nothing was ever reported about Kate dining anywhere in the hotel, it is likely that she took some of her meals in the Crown Room or in the Ladies' Dining Room (three meals a day were included with the price of the room, and it didn't appear as if Kate was bedridden during her entire stay).

On the day Kate Morgan traveled into San Diego, she probably caught the Coronado Railroad "Bay Belt Line" in front of the hotel, headed south down the Strand to the mainland of California and then headed north to San Diego's downtown. In 1892, a trip between the hotel and downtown San Diego cost 60 cents.

The Hotel Del offered some fine technological amenities in 1892, including electricity, elevators and telephones. Although the telephones were not in the guests' rooms, they were probably available for guest use. At that time, however, phones were relatively rare, which explains why the hotel notified the San Diego coroner via telegraph.

Elevators, too, were rare in 1892. In fact, even though the hotel did have elevators, it still followed standard turn-of-the-century hotel pricing, whereby the most expensive rooms were located on the first floor (no stairs to climb), and the least expensive rooms were located on the top floor (where there were the most stairs to climb). After elevators came into widespread use in America, this kind of pricing was discontinued. Kate's room, being on the third floor, was probably not as plush as some, but she clearly did not have the least expensive room in the house. Room rates varied between $3 and $5 per day, depending upon the length of one's stay (the longer the stay, the better the daily rate). Also determining rates were the time of year (off-season rates were lower), the view and whether the room included a private bathroom or not. Kate's room cost $3.80 per day.

Perhaps the hotel's most important technological asset was electricity. In fact, this – as much as anything – may be responsible for the hotel's longevity. In the late 1800s, fires destroyed many Victorian resorts. Dependent on gaslight and a live flame, accidents were plentiful, and resorts burned to the ground on a regular basis. Electricity saved The Del from this fate, although it was not in widespread use around the country until the 1900s.

The electrician who found Kate's body had been "trimming" the exterior electric lights. In the years before electricity, trimming the lights would have meant trimming the wicks on a candle or a gas lamp. The phraseology remained, although it is probable that the electrician was simply turning off the lights by hand which may have involved climbing up the light pole to reach the fixture.

After Kate's death, it was widely reported that Kate's husband, Tom, was a gambler. If he was, he might have traveled the rails to pursue his vocation. In the latter part of the 1800s, train travel and gambling were so intertwined that a deck of cards was referred to as the "railroad bible." The fact is, train travel – though certainly speedy when compared to horseback or carriage – took a great deal of time (a cross-country trip took seven days), so there was plenty of opportunity to play cards – and plenty of opportunity for professional "cardsharps" (this was the Victorian term for cardsharks) to earn their livings; the game of choice was often "three-card monte."

CHAPTER 9

Ghostly Guest Encounters at The Del:
The Spirit of Kate Morgan Lives On

Through the years, hotel guests and employees have reported a variety of ghostly activities in Room 3327 (this is the room Kate Morgan stayed in, although it was numbered 302 at that time). Activity has also been reported in Room 3519, although there is no known connection between Room 3519 and Kate Morgan.

In the recent past, the resort's heritage department has documented ghostly guest encounters.

~

Terrifying Tales

MR. & MRS. R, LAKE ELSINORE, CA
Room 3327
February 2000

Mrs. R and her husband decided to spend a long Valentine's weekend at The Del. Unfortunately, the Victorian Building (where they had wanted to stay) was completely sold out, except for the first night of their planned weekend getaway. As a result, the Rs made reservations for one night in the Victorian Building and the remaining nights in the hotel's Ocean Towers.

The day Mr. and Mrs. R checked in had been rainy and cold, which made their room even more inviting, so they decided to stay in and order room service.

Later that evening, a hotel manager came by to ask them if anything had been inadvertently left in their bathroom (possibly by a hotel employee). The male manager was accompanied by a female housekeeper. While the manager went to check out the bathroom, the housekeeper kept her distance, peering into the room from the hallway.

After dinner, Mrs. R took a shower, where she noticed that the bathroom lights were dimming and flickering off and on. After her shower, Mr. R took a shower. While he was showering, Mrs. R noticed that the tassel on the room's ceiling fan began circulating "as if someone had walked by and brushed it."

Later on – while both Mr. and Mrs. R were in bed asleep – their bedcovers were jerked off the bed (Mrs. R, who thought her husband was just hogging the blankets, went right back to sleep). In the morning, Mr. R asked his wife, "Did you see what happened here last night?" Mrs. R had no idea what her husband was talking about. He then told her that their covers had been pulled off by someone standing at the foot of the bed, where he could see the outline of a female head and body. To make matters worse, as he was lying in bed – too afraid to go back to sleep – Mr. R began hearing the guestroom doorknob rattling. Though he felt drawn to find out what was causing the noise, Mr. R couldn't bring himself to go to the door.

Only after Mr. R told his story did Mrs. R tell her husband about having seen the room's fan tassel moving inexplicably the night before. Imagine Mrs. R's surprise when her husband then told her that he had witnessed a similar thing after she had fallen asleep – he told her that the fan tassel began to move as if someone had walked by and batted it.

Perplexed by these events, Mr. and Mrs. R said a little prayer for what they imagined was the "troubled spirit" in Room 3327. Afterward they called a hotel bellman to help move them into their Ocean Towers room for the remainder of their stay. When the bellman arrived, he greeted them by saying, "Well, what was it like to sleep in the haunted room?" And that was the first either one of them had ever heard anything about a Hotel del Coronado ghost! (Mrs. R later reasoned that the hauntedness may have explained the housekeeper's unwillingness to come into the room the night before, preferring to wait in the hallway instead.)

Curiously, Mrs. R later reported that she had had one of the most peaceful night's sleep in her entire life in Room 3327. She remembers having "wonderful dreams" with "children's laughter." And although Mr. and Mrs. R were more saddened than unnerved by their experiences in Room 3327, they admitted that they have no intention of ever staying in that room again.

A postscript: Three weeks after their Del visit, as Mr. and Mrs. R were recalling the strange goings-on they experienced at The Del, the phone rang. It was a call from San Diego's Old Globe Theatre, informing Mr. and Mrs. R that they had been chosen as the grand-prize winners in a contest. The prize? A trip for two to the Hotel del Coronado. The Rs were thrilled, but when they made their reservations, they made it very clear that they were willing to stay in "any room except 3327."

~

WW, SAN DIEGO, CA
Room 3327
January 2000

A doorman, WW, along with a female concierge, had the opportunity to show off the haunted room to two young guests. After they arrived in the room, WW noticed that the bedcovers needed straightening. It was obvious that a woman had been lying on one side of the bed and had not straightened the covers after she had gotten up. This, in itself, struck WW as very odd, since the room had been thoroughly cleaned and was in every way ready for its next guests.

WW walked over to the bed to straighten out the covers, but when he tried to fix them, he couldn't undo the impression of the woman's body. The guests – as well as the concierge – began screaming, and everyone immediately left the room! Says WW, "I was totally baffled."

About the two young visitors, WW says, "They were a little scared, but they were also very mystified and intrigued about what they had witnessed."

~

CCM, MOORESVILLE, NC
Beach
September 1993

CCM, who is an anesthetist by profession, was living in Minnesota in September 1993, when she made her first trip to The Del. She stayed in a suite in the Victorian Building, at the western corner, facing the ocean, on the second or third floor.

After a lovely dinner in the Crown Room, CCM retired for the night. In the middle of the night – as she often did – CCM got up from bed to get a drink of water. As she was idly looking out the window, CCM noticed a woman walking down some exterior stairs toward the ocean. CCM assumed the woman was in "period costume" since she was wearing a white blouse with a long dark skirt. Her hair was also long and dark. All of a sudden, the woman turned around and looked directly at CCM. CCM was taken aback, wondering how it was possible that the lady on the beach could look directly into the hotel room. CCM's room was in total darkness; there were no lights on, and there was no way for the woman on the beach to be able to see CCM, yet CCM knew that the woman was looking right at her. The experience was so "unnerving" that CCM mentioned it to her future husband the next day.

That same day, as her future husband was checking out, CCM went into the hotel gift shop to purchase some postcards. There she saw a book about the hotel, with a picture of a woman who looked just like the woman CCM had seen the night before. CCM purchased the book, but really didn't think any more about it until she started to thumb through the book about two days later.

The book CCM purchased – which tells the story of Kate Morgan – contained specific information about where Kate's body was found. Only then did CCM realize that the woman she had seen – looking just like Kate Morgan – was also "walking in Kate's footsteps." That's when CCM realized that she may have seen a ghost!

In retrospect, CCM believes that her middle-of-the-night state of mind ("when you wake up in the middle of the night, you don't have your defense mechanisms up") made her more receptive to a ghostly encounter. Although CCM did not know ahead of time that The Del had a resident ghost, CCM does believe in the possible existence of paranormal phenomena.

~

KL, IRVINE, CA
Entering a room located at the back of the hotel
June 1982

KL was part of a four-couple group that was celebrating the 35th birthday of one of their friends. After dinner in town, the eight friends walked back to the hotel.

When KL got to her guestroom at The Del, she glanced at the door next to hers and saw a beautiful woman there. KL says, "I glanced. She glanced. I smiled. She smiled. I went into my room. She went into her room."

Immediately upon entering her room, however, KL suddenly realized that she had seen something special. Unfortunately, when KL looked in the hallway again, the vision had vanished.

"The woman was beautiful with her dark hair pulled up in the back. She was wearing a beautiful dress – fitted waist, high collar, tucks down the front, with sheer sleeves, in a voilelike fabric. But there was no color to her or her clothes. It was all sort of whitish-gray and almost transparent. It was as if there was no life."

KL wasn't sad or scared about the apparition. Instead, she remembers a wonderful "peaceful feeling." Only afterward did KL realize that she had just seen a ghost.

KL had been studying metaphysics at the time, and she feels that she was particularly open to the spiritual world at that point in her life. Five years later, KL did come across a book that featured The Del's ghost, but up until then, she was unaware that The Del had a ghost. She says, "People may imagine that ghosts are always sad, but the Kate I saw was happy."

KL's drawing of Kate is on page 55.

~

Additional Occurrences

Room 3327
1999, 2000, 2001

When a computer executive from the East Coast made his first reservation at The Del in 1999, he asked to stay in the haunted room. Although this guest never saw Kate during his visit, he did experience endlessly quirky events, most of them having to do with failed electrical systems.

First off, each time this gentleman tried to confirm his reservation, he was told that there was no reservation for him in the computer (fortunately, the hotel was always able to retrieve the reservation "manually"). For instance, when he called a week before his stay: "no reservation." When he called from an airport en route to San Diego, the same response. And even after he arrived at The Del and tried to check in: "no reservation."

His Del room keys, which are electronic, failed again and again and again and had to be reprogrammed and reissued a number of times. The lights in his room also dimmed and grew brighter repeatedly, with no apparent explanation.

Upon hearing these stories, a coworker suggested that the gentleman "challenge" the ghost by telling it something like, "If you're really a ghost, let me see you throw a towel into the bathtub!" Though the gentleman in 3327 ignored this suggestion, later that day, a towel mysteriously appeared in the middle of his bathtub; the next day, the same thing happened.

At the end of his 1999 stay, the gentleman was unable to access the hotel's televised check-out system and had to go to the front desk to conduct his final bit of business.

During his 2000 visit in the ghost room, this same gentleman experienced exasperating phone problems. Every day – sometimes more than once a day – his phone would ring, he would answer it, and there would be absolutely nothing there, no sound of someone hanging up, no dial tone, etc. His phone message light would also come on even when there was no message. During the last night of his stay, his phone rang at 4 a.m.; he answered it and there was no one there so he shouted at Kate to cease and desist. With that, the electric alarm clock rang exactly three times. Not only hadn't the alarm clock been set to go off, if it had been set to go off, it would have done so at 6:30 a.m., not 4 a.m.

Finally, during his most recent stay in 2001, he recalls this eerie experience: "When I checked into the room, there was the very clear imprint of someone lying on the bed." The phone also continued to give him problems in 2001: it rang and no one was there, or the message light wouldn't come on when he actually had a message. In addition, problems with electric lights continued to plague him – they turned off and on by themselves; or, after leaving his room with the lights left on, he would return to find them turned off.

As a sidenote, he and his wife stayed in Room 3519 during a 1999 visit. One morning they awoke to find freshly cut roses outside their door with no note or explanation.

~

Room 3327
February 2000

A guest heard moaning and crying in the middle of the night, and wrote on his guest comment card, "Kate Morgan woke us both up with her crying – scary, but interesting!" He also says that immediately after his stay, his pager has been reporting calls from number 3327.

~

Room 3327
1993

Guests reported that the television set suddenly turned itself off, and the television cabinet doors abruptly closed.

~

Room 3519
1992

Christopher Chacon, who is a parapsychologist and the director of the Office of Scientific Investigation and Research in Los Angeles, stayed in Rooms 3327 and 3519. Using infrared cameras and equipment that monitors radio activity, magnetic fields, emissions and temperature and humidity fluctuations, Chacon and his crew were unable to detect any activity in Room 3327. However, they did find 37 abnormalities in Room 3519 and classified that room as a "classic haunting."

~

Room 3519
1992

According to 1992 "Home Show" segment.

The "Home Show" filmed the 1992 Chacon visit, during which an ashtray moved, a lamp moved and a glass shattered on the bathroom floor.

~

Room 3519
1992

According to 1993 People Magazine *article*
(A first-person account of the Chacon October 1992 visit appeared in the September 20, 1993 edition of People Magazine*).*

According to ghost-buster partner, Peter Aykroyd, the Office of Scientific Investigation and Research is a 300-member organization that employs a variety of high-tech tools including night vision goggles, radiation sensors, toxic-chemical indicators, high-frequency sound detectors and a microwave imaging system. During their stay in Room 3519, Aykroyd says they saw a lamp move of its own accord, and that a glass fell and smashed on the floor.

~

Room 3327
October 1992

According to October 1992 San Diego Woman *article and November 1992* San Diego Union-Tribune *article.*

When writer Sharon Whitley stayed in the Kate Morgan room, a towel she had not used became rumpled and smeared with lipstick; lights flickered inexplicably; visiting friends told her that they felt as if someone was watching them, while friends she spoke with on the phone complained of static and the feeling that someone was "listening in." Whitley also had trouble getting into her locked room (and eventually requested a duplicate key). In addition, visiting friends reported that they had heard voices coming from Whitley's empty room (the noises stopped abruptly after they knocked on the door).

Room 3519
1983

According to 1992 interview with former hotel public relations director.

According to a 1992 nationally televised interview, when a Secret Service agent was assigned to Room 3519 in 1983, during George Bush's vice presidency, he called the front desk to complain about the noise from the room above (loud footsteps and talking). When the attendant at the front desk told the agent that there was no room above his room (he was on the top floor), the Secret Service agent asked to change rooms.

~

Activity in Other Rooms

Not all activity can be traced to Kate Morgan or to Rooms 3327 or 3519.

Lobby Area
Dates Uncertain

For instance, some of the concierge staff members have reported hearing muffled conversations that come from nowhere, as well as the sound of young girls whispering. One of the staff members twice sighted a "dusty"-looking fellow (dressed in 1940s-style clothes) who literally disappeared into thin air.

~

Hotel Gift Shops
2001

After an extensive restoration effort, employees in one of the hotel's gift shops started experiencing the supernatural. A salesperson reported that books started "jumping" off the shelves, a sales sign was slammed down on the counter, a clock fell off the wall twice and another clock flew off the shelf it was on (in all cases, there were shoppers in the store at the time who also witnessed the strange goings-on). Another employee also reported that postcards and a book "flew off" (not just fell off) a shelf. In a second shop, a third employee also witnessed jumping books.

~

Room 3284
October 2001

A couple spending their wedding anniversary at The Del experienced a variety of mysterious events. At about 4 a.m. one morning, the television suddenly turned on; another day it changed channels by itself. One night, the wife woke to see about six human apparitions in the room, "all laughing and having a good time." They were dressed in old-fashioned clothes, the men wearing suspenders and one woman in a bonnet. The next day, her husband confirmed what his wife had seen (he had been awakened by the same group, but not at the same time).

~

Room 3343
1999

A family staying in this room witnessed their mother's strange reflection in the bathroom mirror, where her eyes were the size of Orphan Annie's (two or three times their normal size), and each appeared to be configured like a bull's eye.

~

Room 3517
December 1998

A seamstress was working with a local theatre group, which was putting together a production at The Del; Room 3517 was being used as the wardrobe room. After an exhausting day – which had begun early in the morning and ended well past midnight – the seamstress fell asleep (a coworker had already fallen asleep in the room).

At about 3 a.m. – shortly after the seamstress had gone to bed – she heard a loud knocking on a nearby coffee table but she figured the noise must have been coming from a nearby room. Then her headboard began knocking (again, she figured it must have been caused by a commotion in the room next door). She yelled, "Stop that! Leave me alone!" – and the knocking ceased.

Very early the next morning, she heard a voice whisper, "Get up; you've got to see this" (unbeknownst to her, her sleeping coworker had received the very same message). At any rate, they both went to the window to see a spectacular sunrise (the seamstress was normally a late riser and not used to seeing the sunrise). Only later did the two women realize that neither one of them had spoken, yet each had heard the same thing, and each had been drawn to look out the window.

~

Room Numbers Unknown

We also sometimes get feedback from guests well after their stays, in which case exact room numbers cannot always be determined.

2000

After their visit, a couple reported the sound of a radio alarm in the connecting room – only to find out that that room had not been occupied. The husband also saw the apparition of a "thin woman in a white smocked gown, with a long, oval face and light blond hair to her shoulders," who appeared in their guestroom and then "promptly disappeared."

~

June 1999

A doctor staying at the hotel wrote to The Del after his visit describing his nightly ritual of neatly placing his socks and shoes together before going to bed. During his stay at The Del, however, he woke to find that one of his socks was a good ten feet from his shoes (with no possible explanation!).

~

1992

A nine-year-old girl remembers waking up during the night to see a transparent woman in a white nightgown standing near her bed.

~

Date Unknown

Another couple reported seeing the ghost of a "beautiful blond girl dressed in layered and tapered cream chiffon," who floated between them in their guestroom.

3327

Chapter 10

Kate Morgan the Ghost:
What the Experts Say

Not everyone believes in ghosts, but for those who have experienced the supernatural, ghosts are very, very real.

Ghosts have been a part of spoken and written language since the beginning of time. And the popularity of "ghost stories" doesn't appear to be waning – a year doesn't go by without the release of at least one scary "supernatural" movie. Though ghosts have been around forever, the way people perceive them does change over time and across cultures (for instance, Iceland reports many ghosts; Hong Kong reports very few).

Although many people think of ghosts as something akin to the white-sheeted variety we see on Halloween, parapsychologists (who study the supernatural) report that ghosts can actually appear in a myriad of forms – from spooky skeletons to vague "watery" images to completely lifelike human beings; animal ghosts have also been reported. Some ghosts move around, communicate (although sometimes "conversation" takes place without words), or make physical contact with their observer. Ghosts can appear anywhere and at all hours of the day and night.

Some people believe that a ghost is the physical manifestation of a human spirit, which separates from the body at the time of death. Others believe that the past can somehow intersect with the present, whereby the living can interact with the deceased.

Many researchers believe that an especially sudden or violent death can cause a spirit – in the form of a ghost – to be left behind. Although Kate Morgan's death doesn't appear to have been particularly sudden, she was very young, and she may have made the decision to take her own life only days or hours before she committed the act. In any event, Kate's death was definitely violent. And the dramatic circumstances surrounding Kate's life – all alone and without a home to speak of – also add to the extreme circumstances of her suicide.

Some paranormal experts believe that when someone dies tragically – even by their own hand – he or she may be unable to accept their own death. Instead, the person remains tied to earth, perhaps in an attempt to take care of some unfinished business.

Guests and employees alike have tried to answer the question: "Why does Kate Morgan's spirit remain at The Del?" Some think she is still waiting for her husband, Tom, to join her. Others believe that without family and a permanent home, she has nowhere else to go. Still others believe that Kate doesn't want to leave The Del, that she likes "living" here (as one guest pointed out, what better place than the Hotel del Coronado to spend eternity!).

Although not all ghosts inhabit old buildings (and not all old buildings have ghosts), Kate's circumstances are somewhat typical – her ghost inhabits the place where she long ago died.

In past sightings, Kate Morgan has sometimes appeared as a real human being, dressed in period clothes, looking so real that some observers haven't always realized they were seeing a ghost until after the vision had passed. In these instances, Kate sometimes looks "solid," but other times she appears to be more pale, or even transparent. Kate has also appeared as a rather indistinct form, looking vaguely like the outline of a woman, or she has left her female "imprint" behind, but has remained invisible.

Some of Kate's paranormal observers have referenced extreme changes in the temperature of Room 3327 (whether or not Kate appeared). Research has shown that severe drops in room temperature (sometimes accompanied by a "chill to the bone") often go hand in hand with ghost sightings. No one has ever seen Kate for an extended time, which is also consistent with paranormal research (ghosts rarely appear for more than few brief seconds). And, just like many other ghost sightings, Kate seems to appear "out of nowhere," and she disappears just as quickly. In these and other ways, Kate is a "typical" ghost.

Sometimes Kate appears to be going about the business of daily life (walking on the beach or entering a room). At other times, Kate directly interacts with observers – for instance, by appearing and then pulling the bedcovers off a bed. In either case, Kate does not appear to be completely oblivious to the people around her (as some ghosts are).

In addition, although some ghosts may appear to have a "mission" on earth, Kate does not seem to fall into this category. She doesn't try to warn or help people; neither does she want to hurt people. At this point, it isn't clear what Kate's purpose is, or even if she has a purpose.

Although quite a few people have seen the ghost of Kate Morgan, there are many others who have only witnessed some supernatural antics, which may or may not be attributable to Kate. There is a subset of paranormal research that focuses on poltergeists, which are invisible forces that can cause objects to move, break or fly across the room. Poltergeists can also produce inexplicable noises, make lights turn on and off, or make doors open and shut.

Much of this kind of activity has been reported in Kate's room, as well as in Room 3519. Is this the work of Kate Morgan – or is this the result of a poltergeist (or poltergeists) unrelated to Kate? Most paranormal experts believe that poltergeists are a short-lived phenomenon, and that they don't "haunt" over the long term. Others believe that poltergeists are caused by strong human emotions "sent out" by the living and have nothing to do with the supernatural. Still other researchers believe that poltergeist activity is the playful work of a "regular" ghost. Interestingly, however, stealing bedcovers – something Kate has been accused of doing – is a "typical" poltergeist activity.

In the last half of the 19th century – during the time Kate was at The Del – there was an increased interest in "spiritualism," which involved communicating with deceased loved ones through a "medium" (someone who was able – or claimed to be able – to talk with the dead). In fact, as early as the mid-1800s, America boasted almost a dozen periodicals on the subject of spiritualism. By the end of the century, spiritualism was part of the mainstream consciousness, though certainly not widely embraced.

Because of America's interest in spiritualism – and everything related to it – ghost sightings during the Victorian era were closely studied and well-documented. As it turns out, Kate's ghost is very similar to the kind of ghost Kate would have read about back in 1892, when most ghosts were described as having varying degrees of human form, were harmless and often without obvious purpose. Interestingly, some of today's scientists believe that the number of ghosts has decreased since the Victorian period because the number of violent, sudden deaths has decreased.

Today, people can be roughly divided into two groups – those who believe in the supernatural and those who don't (some surveys show the split to be about 50%-50%). For those who do believe in ghosts, not all have actually ever seen a ghost – or ever will. For those who would like to experience the supernatural firsthand, ghosts – including Kate – are not very accommodating, and they cannot be conjured up at will.

Some researchers believe that the ability to experience the supernatural varies from person to person. Even for those people who can experience the paranormal, individual differences will exist (some people may have a lot of experiences with lots of different ghosts, while others may have only one sighting over the course of a lifetime).

Here at The Del, we are trying to record – whenever possible – credible accounts of ghostly sightings or paranormal interactions as part of our ongoing historic research. Perhaps one day we will have a better understanding of Kate Morgan's life – and her afterlife.

3327